Who We Are

Heroes & Bullies

Sara Madden

First written in 2006, first published in 2021
This edition published in 2026
www.saramadden.com

ISBN: 978-1-946505-36-1 (Paperback)
ISBN: 978-1-946505-35-4 (eBook)

Printed in the United States of America
10 9 8 7 6 5 4 3 2 1

Cover design by Zaugg Studios
Cover images from Zaugg Studios and @Freepik
Book design and interior layout by Sara Madden
Author photograph: Zaugg Studios

To my grandma, In loving memory
To my grandpa, In loving memory and great admiration
To my dad, In deepest gratitude
To my mom, In loving appreciation

*The legacy of heroes is the memory of a great name and
the inheritance of a great example.*
—Benjamin Disraeli

*The hero draws inspiration from the
virtue of his ancestors.*
—Johann Goethe

Foreword

Dear Reader,

I wrote this story over six weeks during the summer of 2006 for my grandpa. When I decided to publish it for my family, I chose to keep it unedited and unchanged from the version that my grandpa read before he died in 2013, other than a few grammatical changes for publication purposes. My sister designed the book cover, and the photo of the boy is her son, my nephew, who looks like our dad at that age. The character C.E. is based on my dad.

While this book is not a masterpiece, it is a heartfelt story written by a granddaughter to her most beloved grandpa whom she still misses every day.

Thank you for reading.

Sincerely,

Sara

Chapter One

Sometimes, when one person is missing, the whole world seems depopulated. —Alphonse de Lamartine

MY LITTLE MISS, HUSH now. I am here. The woman's faint voice from my dream speaks to me. I stir in my sleep, twisting in my covers. I hear the voice now as an echo of singing. *Soft as the voice of an angel ... Hope for the sunshine tomorrow ... Whispering hope ... Making my heart in its sorrow rejoice.*

I sit up in bed and touch my face with the tips of my fingers. My forehead is damp. I turn and look at the alarm clock. The arms glow at 6:15 a.m., the time of my birth. Today is August 9, 1965, my thirteenth birthday. I grab my chest and try to slow my breathing. The pulse on my wrist is too fast for me to count. I reach to turn on my lamp. My shaky hands fumble as they try to find the cord.

Click, click. Squinting, I look around the room frantically, still gasping for air. The curtains blow in and out of my bedroom window. I check my pulse again. It is slowing down. The thumping in my chest starts to tame.

I nearly faint as I make my way to the window. I cling to the sill and inhale deeply for air as I recall the voice from my dream. *My little miss, hush now. I am here.* It is the voice I imagine my mother had if she had lived past my first minutes of life. Something inside me knows it was her. There was not a figure in my dream, just a gentle wind carrying my mother's voice to me. I do not know if I should feel comforted or jump out of my skin.

I wish I could ask my grandpa what it means to have my mother in my dreams on the morning of my thirteenth birthday. Could I have just created her voice, or did my mind lock away the memory until now? Was the whispering I heard my mother's last breath? Did my mother name me Missy? Grandpa would know.

I sit at my window and watch the sun slowly rise. This is my first birthday without my grandpa. I cannot run to him and ask him my questions about heaven, death, and why I feel so alone at this moment. I will not see him come through the door at 6:15 a.m. on my birthday anymore. This thought overwhelms me, and I wish it were not my birthday today.

It has been a hard year. I lost my Grandpa Howard eleven months ago, and things have been gloomy around the house. My dad did not even return home for the funeral. I have not seen him since I was five. He left me here to be raised by his parents while he "figures out his life." The last thing I remember him telling me was "I'll be back for you soon."

For months I waited for him on the front porch every day after school with my pillowcase packed with my clothes. When the weather turned cold, I would sit at the window, wrapped in my coat, scarf, hat, and mittens, still waiting. By Christmas, I received three postcards from three different continents. When I was ten, I had received more than eighty postcards from around the world. Every time the mail would arrive with a new one, Grandpa would take me to Rexall's drug store for a milkshake to take my mind off my abandonment. But over the years, my grandparents more than made up for my lack of a father.

This is my first birthday without my grandpa's traditional birthday wish speech. Every year, my grandpa would always tell me that I would have an adventurous life. Without him here, I wonder if that will happen. Even though my grandpa always said that this was the best place to live because of the button factory and Sweet Betty Sue, the little town of Ogdenville I live in does not have much to offer. I can hardly expect any adventure to happen to me if I am stuck here.

The house I live in is built into the button factory, with the store across from the front parlor. "You live in a button factory, and your last name is Button! That itself is an adventure," Grandpa would proudly remind me when I couldn't wait for a real adventure to come my way. He would lovingly tap my head and ask, "How much more excitement does one need in a lifetime?"

I will require a lot more now that I am thirteen. What girl does not want to have a death-defying moment, a fairy-tale romance, and friendships worth dying for? Is that too much to ask?

The seventy-three clocks in the house all chime 6:30 at once. When I place my hand on the wall, I can feel the house vibrate. The clocks are a comfort but sometimes a nuisance. The birds scatter as they ring. The clocks remind me that I have an hour before breakfast to sit and reflect on my life, only this year I will do it alone. Grandpa used to recap my entire life the morning of my birthday while we walked around the property. Then he would give me my birthday wish speech before making my favorite breakfast of oatmeal with cranberries and pecans, and brown sugar pancakes with maple syrup. I guess my first responsibility as a teenager is to recount my own life as if my grandpa were still here with me.

I clear my throat and prepare to play my grandpa's role in the recap of my life. How did he start? Oh yeah, he always began with "You're as cute as a button."

My last name is—I mean, my grandpa would say, "Your last name is Button. When our ancestors left Switzerland and arrived in New York in 1865, their last name was Knopf, which in German means 'button.' My grandparents traveled to America with one trunk, two pocket watches, and no direction until they heard of a button factory out west." I visualize him pausing to take out his pipe and hit it against his knee as I wait for the rest of the story. "They took the word button as a sign and traveled west to settle in the town of Ogdenville. Generation after generation of Buttons has worked for and owned this factory while living in this house attached to the front of it for over one hundred years."

He would smile at me, take my shoulder, and say, "One day this will all be yours." I can see him now, his thin silver hair neatly combed, his proud face gleaming while he pointed with his pipe to everything around our property that he thought was wonderful.

I point out the window at each of the things he loved so much. "That whitewashed house with baby blue shutters, the barn, the brick button factory that towers over and protects our home, the tall trees, the geranium lined dirt road ..." He would slowly trail off and look toward town.

"Ah, the covered bridge over Thimble Creek, the train station at the edge of town," I remember last year when he talked about the town, his eyes glistened, and his cheeks turned rosy. He reminded me of a small child at Christmas. There was always love in his voice when he talked about the town.

"A town that offers anything you could ever need. Amazing," he would say, always so grateful for what he had in his life. This is one of the things that I adored about him.

I look out at Ogdenville and try to see it through his eyes. But all I can see are a few statistics that are not very impressive. Ogdenville boasts a population of nearly twenty thousand. If I could see it as he did, I would say, "Ogdenville comprises the eight necessities a town needs: a church, a school, a hospital, a library, a movie theater, a corner market, a drugstore, and a paint store. Not to forget a pretty nice button factory, of course."

I can still hear the singing of Grandpa's pipe being lit and the warm, nutty smell of the smoke that billowed when he would take two puffs before looking down at me.

"Ah, what a blessed life we have," he would say and take my hand. He would finish smoking his pipe as we slowly walked around the property, admiring our family's legacy.

I look at the brick building with its clean, unblemished windows. The factory has not been running for the past twenty years. Production stopped after World War II when everyone started using plastic buttons. Instead of upgrading the equipment to produce plastic buttons, my grandparents decided to shut it down and sell the large stock of buttons they already had. It would be able to resume work tomorrow if we wanted to start producing metal buttons again. We have always kept the factory and the property in good working condition. But since we do not manufacture buttons anymore, we sell vintage and out-of-stock buttons to the four connecting states. Over the past decade, the store has added quilts and sewing notions to its inventory to help pay the property taxes on the factory.

On the front door of our home (which is also the entrance to the store), a sign reads, "If you have lost your marbles, you're at the wrong store. If you have lost a button, please come on in." On the main floor are the button shop, a small parlor, and the kitchen toward the back.

The parlor is where Sweet Betty Sue loves to sit and knit when she is not helping a customer or baking in the kitchen. Lately, she has been knitting light and dark blue squares for the afghan she started for my grandpa before he died. She sits with her knitting needles clicking two or three times, and then she stops. She believes in always finishing projects that she starts, but I can tell she is having a hard time finishing this project for my grandpa. She has never walked away from a project, and I don't think she will start with these squares. She will just take a very long time to finish them.

My sorrow is deep with my grandpa gone, but my Sweet Betty Sue and he were married for fifty years. She is a very quiet and private woman, but I can tell her heart is bleeding, just as deep as mine.

"On the second floor is your room. It is your dad's old room. It looks the same as it did when he was eight," Grandpa would say, continuing with my life story.

The room still has my dad's model airplanes hanging from the ceiling, which Grandpa always pointed out because he had helped my dad make them. The toy trains on shelves were Christmas presents, and the microscope on the desk and the telescope by the window were bought by my dad himself. Grandpa would say, "It made us so proud the day your daddy purchased those with his own money from working the ice cream counter at Rexall's drugstore."

The walls still have green plaid wallpaper. My bed has an iron headboard with baseballs painted on it. There is a broken kite in the corner that says, "Girls stink!" Seven old school books with unfinished homework tucked inside are stacked on the desk. Three of the books always seemed out of place with his science and math books: *The Oxford Book of Poetry, Shakespeare Unabridged,* and *The Com-*

plete Works of Emily Dickinson. Maybe he took literature in high school so that he could be with my mom.

The green and blue striped pajamas I am wearing, and half of my wardrobe even belonged to my dad. I do not have much to claim as my own. I have my dog, my red bandana, my jar of buttons, and my bike.

Feeling exhausted with weak legs, I walk back to my bed and curl under the covers to finish what my grandpa would have said if he were here. I smooth the covers and clear my voice once more.

"The red Afghan your mom knitted for you before you were born covers your entire bed. It started as a small baby blanket, but at the end of her pregnancy and her life, she just kept knitting until you were born. I believe the clicking of her needles calmed her down during her last few days alive." I wrap my arms around my knees and pull the red Afghan over my body.

I can feel my grandpa's sympathy even now. He was always tender and sweet when he got to the part about Mom. He would take a moment to sit me on the fence and look out at the sunrise. He would squeeze my hand and finish telling me about the day I was born.

"She wrapped you in that red afghan moments after you were born, and you fell asleep in her arms before she passed." He would wipe his eyes and look at my face. "The moment you were placed in your mom's arms was the happiest she had ever had in her life, even if it only lasted for eighty-six seconds."

Every year when he told me that story, I got chills all over my arms. Now with her voice in my dream, the chills run up my neck. "When you turned five, we brought you home to the button factory and raised you into the fine young girl you are today," Grandpa would finish before planting a kiss on my forehead.

A dog barks outside, and I climb out of bed and look out the side window, which overlooks the barn and part of the factory. I use my dad's old telescope to investigate the barn to check on Howard, my dog, to make sure he isn't harassing the livestock.

I play with the telescope and run my fingers over my dad's initials, DLB. Daniel Lion Button. I look around my room, which makes me feel safe and close to my parents. I feel like I am home with them when I am alone in my room. This room is my connection to my dad and contains the only picture of my parents together.

The picture is on my nightstand. They were high school sweethearts. My grandpa told me that he took this picture of them after my mom and dad's State Debate Conference, where they won first place with their team. My dad makes bunny ears behind my mom's head as she shields her eyes from the sun with her hand. Dad is laughing, and Mom is looking to the side. Her other hand is placed over the large bouquet of daisies on her lap. There is a trophy at her feet that reaches to her knees with the year 1943 inscribed. Everything I know about my mom is either in this picture or in the story of my Afghan.

I hope one day to have a sweetheart, but not until I am much older; maybe when I turn fourteen. C.E. says people in love have rocks in their heads. I do not take his opinion too seriously because he also says that bullies have rocks in their heads. I can't help but smile at C.E.'s opinions about rocks.

I move to the other window in my room to see C.E.'s house with the telescope. I can make out morning cartoons through the front room window. Knowing that he is watching *Casper the Friendly Ghost* makes me smile.

C.E. is my very best friend. His dad is the handyman around the factory and our property. They live just across Thimble Creek, which runs along the train tracks where he and I place pennies. Other than fishing at the creek, we spend most of our time in C.E.'s tree house. We do everything together.

His initials stand for Cornelius Everblot, and his last name is Zog. He hates his name. He would blame his mom, but she ran off when he was two days old. Corny was his nickname for a few years, but he changed it to C.E. because he got beat up more often over the nickname "Corny" than for his actual name. He believes that the reason he is bullied so much is because of his name.

C.E. does indeed get bullied a lot, but I do not think his name is the reason. He just does not stand up for himself. No matter what anyone says, he continues to blame it on his name. I wish he would go by Cornelius. It sounds like a very dashing name. If I told him I thought that way about his name, he would legally have it changed. And I would bet a gazillion million dollars that he would change it to Clark Kent.

Just last month, the Bennett brothers went and pulled all the daisy heads off their stems in his dad's garden. Dine, C.E.'s dad, came out and asked why they would do such a thing. Those Bennett brothers told Dine that C.E. had done it. He did not stick up for himself and took the blame. He was grounded from the tree house for a week and had to shovel turkey poop into the garden and plant more daisies.

What is worse than his punishment was that he fell into a shallow ditch and landed on a patch of poison ivy after losing control of the wheelbarrow. I dabbed calamine lotion on his arms and face for a week. Whenever I see anything with pink polka dots, I'm always reminded of the hives on C.E.'s face and arms.

I know C.E. has courage inside of him somewhere. I wonder sometimes how deep down in there it is because I have never seen anyone so scared to live their life. I believe that one day he will do something amazing; he will amaze even himself.

The clocks chime at seven o'clock. I watch from my window as Howard runs into the house; then I turn to pull my overalls from the hook on the wall when I smell a beautiful aroma. While I get dressed, I see that the honeysuckle has climbed up to my window and wonder why I have not noticed it before. The summer morning breeze makes the air taste sweet. It makes me hungry for dessert. Well, everything makes me hungry for dessert.

After every Sunday dinner, we eat the same dessert, angel food cake. This is my Sweet Betty Sue's way of showing me that she loves me, and I always look forward to it each week. Tonight, I will get one candle on it for my birthday and maybe even some sprinkles. C.E. and Dine will come for dinner. I always look forward to the fresh-cut daisies Dine gives me every year on my birthday. Daisies are such happy flowers. The thought of them makes me glad that it's my birthday today.

Howard barks in Sweet Betty Sue's parlor. The last time he got into the parlor, he knocked over her curio cabinet and broke three teacups in her collection. I had to paint the barn as punishment. It took C.E. and me two weeks to paint it and another three months to glue those cups back together. I still cannot look at those teacups without feeling I could have done a better job.

There are not two teacups alike. My grandpa would purchase a teacup for Sweet Betty Sue every time he went away on business. He would always come home with a teacup and say, "There is only one Sweet Betty Sue in the world." She has thirty teacups in her collection. Some are covered in flowers, some have swirly patterns, some are tall, and some are wide. The one she liked the most was broken, so I kept one piece of it in my button jar. The porcelain piece is dark green with part of red geranium.

I pick up my jar of buttons and baubles from my windowsill. I have collected buttons and other small mementos over the years. Everything in the jar contains a memory that I hold dear.

I have a button from each outfit I wore on my first days of school. There is a button from the rain slicker I borrowed from Sweet Betty Sue's best friend, Dandelion. I even have a button from my orthodontist's lab coat. But my favorite is the one I pulled from Lizzie Bennett's doll bonnet in second grade.

There are at least eighty buttons in here, as well as a piece of the broken teacup, an empty matchbox, C.E.'s old lenses from the glasses he wore in the fourth grade, my tiger eye marbles, and the first tooth I ever lost. I hope that this year I will gather even more memories. But this year I will ask for the buttons instead of just taking them.

I did not realize I had been stealing until the people whose buttons I took came into the store looking for re-placements. Sweet Betty Sue knows about my collection, and she always gives them free buttons. The last time I took a button and she had to replace it, she turned to me at the register, gave me a sympathetic smile, and said, "Just ask them next time, OK?"

I snap the button on the front pocket of my overalls and try to make myself look presentable for breakfast. I study my face in the mirror. I look at my almond-shaped and slanted eyes and wonder what my mom looked like at my age. I recall her voice from my dream now. "My little miss, hush now. I am here."

I hold up the picture of her next to my face, but it is too small and blurry to make a comparison. I wonder if she had eleven freckles across her nose as I do. I bet she did not name the one under her right eye Molly the way I have. I smile a large, toothy grin at my reflection and wonder if she wore braces too. Was her favorite color red as mine is? Did she have brown straight hair too? I wish I had a button of hers for my jar.

My stomach lurches as I realize what I want for my birthday: something of my mother's. A ribbon she wore in her hair as a child, buttons from her prom dress, a dried flower from her wedding bouquet. Anything.

I wonder if C.E. bought me another comic book this year. Maybe I should seek adventure through comics like he does rather than expect too much to happen to me just because I turned thirteen today.

The birthday wishes speech my grandpa would have given after recapping my life echoes in my head. "Seek out who you are. Create your adventures. And I will always be proud of you, Little Miss."

I take the red bandana that Grandpa gave me on my sixth birthday and tie it around my head. My heart triple beats, and I am forced to sit on the edge of my bed. I tie my shoes just as the clocks chime at 7:30.

I feel a sense of yearning for knowledge and adventure this year. Does this mean I am growing up? Maybe this means I am old enough for pierced ears.

I woke up this morning with a change inside of me. I want to find out about my mom. I hope that I am like her in some small way when I do learn about her.

As the newest teenager on the planet, I feel like I can make some demands for the upcoming year. I guess you can call it growth, but what I want instead of clothes and toys this year is for the weight on my heart from the loss of my grandpa to turn to comfort. I want the anger from his absence to dissolve into peace. I want to find happiness in the things that used to bring him joy.

I will always carry my love for my grandpa with me. I know that he is still a part of me, but I am amid an identity crisis now that he is gone. I still feel his love for me and cherish the special gift he gave me every year, recapping my life and giving me my birthday wish speech.

I head for the stairs.

I am ready to be thirteen.

I am ready for what awaits me.

I am ready to become someone in this world.

Chapter Two

The opportunities for heroism are limited in this kind of world: the most people can do is sometimes not to be so weak as they've been at other times. —Agnes Wilson

LAST NIGHT DURING DINNER I could tell that my Sweet Betty Sue wanted to chastise me. Howard got into her parlor while I was getting ready yesterday and knocked the curio over again, breaking two more teacups. I guess that since it was my birthday yesterday, she did not feel she should punish me. But today, as I help prepare the store for business, I also prepare myself for a scolding.

The phone rings, and I offer to answer it, but after the second ring, it stops. The doorbell clangs, and I run to open it, only to find that the mail carrier has left a package on the porch. When I walk back into the store, Sweet Betty Sue is smoothing down her apron.

"Missy Lou, that dog is not allowed in my parlor," she says as she continues to mark inventory of the button case in the Gold, French, and Early 19th Century Buttons section. "I think the front door and the shutters need a new coat of baby blue paint, don't you?" She is smoothing her apron front again and places her hands in the pockets. She looks to me for a response and waits.

Painting is always my punishment for not keeping an eye on my dog. "Yes, I think that is a great idea. Why don't I paint them for you?" I say in return. She smiles and pushes her glasses up on her nose. Adjusting her brooch, she turns to help the first customer of the day over at the antiquities rack.

I'm walking to the door with the broom when Ms. Tovah Stein from the historical society runs into me, and I fall to the ground fast. It is not hard to see why bumping into Ms. Tovah Stein would level anyone to the floor. She is six foot four and has long red hair, gapped front teeth, and the largest, most magnificent personality and booming voice.

"Well, what are you doing on the floor, Missy?" she asks, laughing. I take her large hand, and she pulls me right to my feet.

"Good morning, Ms. Tovah Stein. It's always a pleasure running into you." She is still laughing, and for a moment, I believe I can feel the earth shake.

"Come help me with my buttons before you take off," she says and wraps her arm around my neck, dragging me to the counter.

I pull out her order of antique buttons, and she waits with her arms resting on the counter. The noise from her twenty or thirty bracelets startles everyone in the store, but it does not seem to bother her. She pulls her large black sunglasses off and hooks them on her plunging neckline.

While I count all forty buttons and place them in a paper bag, she rummages through her purse and discreetly slides over a little package. She places her finger on her lips and rolls her eyes in my grandma's direction. I open it quietly while Ms. Tovah Stein makes small talk about my birthday.

"Did you get sprinkles on your cake this year? How were the daisies from Dine? What did C.E. get you this year?" she asks as I hurry to open my gift after my Sweet Betty Sue looks over at us.

I answer each question, "Yes. Beautiful. A tackle box." Ms. Tovah Stein pulls the wrapper from the counter and puts it in her purse quickly. "Cherry red lipstick!" I exclaim. "Thank you!" She places her finger on my mouth now, and I mouth the words to her this time. "Thank you!"

"You can only wear it in the bathroom or the barn. You're not old enough to wear it to school, and I know your grandma won't approve of it at home." She shakes my shoulders. "Promise?" I hand her the bag of buttons, and she peeks inside.

"These buttons are going to look simply lovely on my costume," she says in an extravagant accent. "I hope to see you at the festival and dance this year, Missy Lou."

"I wouldn't miss it for anything," I say. "What song are you singing?"

"'Sylvia.' Always 'Sylvia.'" She puckers her lips and blows me a kiss at the door, and I wave goodbye.

I look around the store to make sure everyone is occupied before I duck behind the register. I pull out the drawer of all our specialty orders to look at the pearl buttons Sweet Betty Sue ordered for a customer.

Out of all the buttons I have ever seen, and I have seen a lot, these are my favorite. They are simple, sweet, elegant, and have just the right amount of shine. Best of all, they are encircled with the most delicate rhinestones, which I pretend are diamonds. Sweet Betty Sue clears her throat loudly, and I put them back.

I dust the store, beginning with the framed catalog of the first *National Button Bulletin* from 1938. Sweet Betty Sue and her quilting club are the only ones left in the universe that still meet as the Button, Button, Who's Got the Button Society. I learn everything about anything at those meetings, which are also held at the same time as their quilting club. I have learned from them the ten pieces it takes to make a button, from the shank to the decorative ring, as well as why if just one piece is missing, a button simply isn't a button. Sometimes I feel as if I am a button missing a piece.

The next frame I dust is as large as the decorative mirror hanging over the fireplace in the parlor. It holds small, silver dollar-sized buttons with every Button ancestor immortalized on each one, starting with the first Buttons to leave Switzerland: Leslie and Mathilda Knopf. There's a button with Great Aunt Mary, who could ride a cow; a button with Great Grandpa Norm, who grew a beard down to his waist but had to cut it off when it got caught in the factory equipment. There is even one with my grandpa's sister, Arvella, who once held eight golf balls in her mouth without flinching.

At the end of the long rectangular frame is a button with my Grandpa Howard. I rub the cloth over his face and catch a glimpse of my reflection. I whisper, "Grandpa." I smile back at his mischievous grin; the same one he would give me after teasing me.

I remember him laughing behind me one time as I played marbles on the driveway. "Quick, look over there!" he said.

I turned to him, and he was smoking his pipe, looking at his watch. He glanced back at me and said, "What?" I returned to my game of marbles, and he started laughing again. Quickly, I turned to see what he was laughing about. He made a straight face and repeated, "What?"

By the fourth time of this back and forth, I ran and hopped on his lap, and he tickled me. His hearty chuckle shook me. "Gotcha, my little Nutmeg," he said. We used to spend hours playing marbles on those days.

I let out a small, sad laugh as I remembered my grand-pa's nickname for me. I look back at his picture and whis-per "Grandpa" again. I can hear his voice whisper back, "Nutmeg." I give the glass one more good swipe to make sure the dust is gone and hear a customer clear their throat. I turn to the counter.

"Those are the smallest frames I have ever seen," she says, placing a button card next to the register.

I write her order on a slip and hand it to her. "They are called tintypes or ferrotypes but are buttons. They were popular around the 1860s through the turn of the century." She hands me a ten bill, and I make the change.

"Many soldiers used them as an inexpensive way to carry pictures of loved ones to war. They were also used and produced as political campaign buttons," I continue after I have completed the sale. I look up at the customer and she raises her eyebrows and politely smiles.

"Amazing. Thanks for the interesting facts about the buttons," she says sweetly. She heads for the door and tells Sweet Betty Sue that I need a hobby of my own instead of working around buttons.

I slam the register drawer closed and move to the other side of the store to clean up the buttons in the Art Nouveau section. These buttons start at twelve dollars apiece and climb to two hundred. We rarely have customers purchase them, but they do browse through them and leave them in the wrong place. Every time I sort them, I spend my time looking at each one, trying to learn more about Sweet Betty Sue's brooch that she always wears. I know it is a button, but that is all I know. I believe it comes from this era, possibly between the years 1890 and 1910.

"Excuse me, Missy?" a small voice says from behind me. I turn and see Penny Copperfield pushing her glasses up her nose. She stands as if she is ashamed to have bothered me.

"Oh, hi, Penny," I say, completely shocked to see her outside of school. "Um. What can I help you with?" I ask because I cannot think of another conversation starter. Penny and I rarely talk at school, and whenever we are paired up on an assignment, we never talk about anything but the topic that we are assigned.

She opens her handbag and drops it accidentally. We both bend down and start picking up its contents. "Oh, I'm sorr-sorr-sorry. I ju-ju-just need a few buttons to finish thi-this project," she says.

I help her up and look at the drawing she has made of an elaborate bracelet made from odds and ends. "My m-mom gave me the challenge to make something ou-out of every-day items one would not necessarily put on a bracelet," she softly says. "I already have a paper clip, a thi-thimble, and now I n-n-need a few buttons. Can you help me find some metal buttons that would match?"

I show her the section of metal and formed buttons. She picks out three very modern swirled buttons, and I write her an invoice at the register.

She slides thirty-five cents across the counter and whis-pers her thanks to me. I watch her leave and wonder why she is so shy. I mean, yes, her name is Penny Copperfield, her hair is as red as copper, and she has copper freckles everywhere. She also has a bit of a stutter, but it has never stopped her from doing anything. She is quite an amazing girl.

I hear someone mention paint across the store, so I stop analyzing Penny and remember that I need to head into town to get paint for the shutters. I hang my apron on the hook and mouth the word paint to Sweet Betty Sue. She nods and excuses herself from the customer she was helping for a moment.

She walks over to the door where I wait. "Don't be gone too long," she says as she straightens my bandana. Her best friend, Dandelion, walks through the front door. "My quilting club meets tonight, and I need help setting up the blocks."

"Nice to see you, dear. I am bringing ginger, date, and chocolate chip cookies for you tonight. Can you pick up some whipped cream to go with it while you're out?" Dandelion asks, pinching my cheeks.

I shake my head and run from the shop out to the barn to get my banana seat bike before I can run into anyone else. Tonight will be full of endless chatter between Sweet Betty Sue, Dandelion, Rosie, Nancy Jo, and Ethel, the county's expert quilters and expert chatters. They are, however, Sweet Betty Sue's oldest and dearest friends. My job is to offer them sweets and cool drinks, to tell them their cookies are fantastic, and to nod my head as they tell me stories.

Maybe tonight they won't ask me to join the circle and stitch my first square on their beautiful quilts. I do not sew and have no interest in sewing. They always promise me it only takes practice, but I tried sewing on a button one time and drew more blood than I care to remember.

However, the quilts they make are exquisite. They can be patriotic, family trees, storytellers, floral bouquets, even animals. They are the most talented women and have the greatest ideas for quilts. They are finishing a quilt for the town festival, which commemorates the city's two hundredth anniversary. I am proud to say that there is a small square with the button factory stitched onto it and that we sell their quilts in our store.

During last week's meeting, they talked about Crystal and how she is such an accomplished seamstress after just eight years of teaching herself. They also mentioned that Ms. Tovah Stein's volunteer work with the historical society has kept the button factory in business. I remember hearing the name Zella and talking of her fragile mental state, but from that point forward, I turned my head to the latest songs from the radio and nodded politely the rest of the evening.

On my way into town, I stop at C.E.'s house. I ride up the front drive and feel as if I'm a fairy floating past the tall zinnias, black-eyed Susans, hollyhocks, and rose bushes of every color that line the path. His house is painted sage green with white shutters. Flower baskets are hanging from all the windows, and they drape down like beautiful locks of hair. I walk toward the front door past the butterfly garden. Howard tries to catch a large orange butterfly. I notice Dine walking out of his greenhouse with a small plant in his hand. As soon as he sees me, he tips his hat at me.

"Good afternoon, Missy Lou and Howard. How have you managed to be thirteen for a whole day?" he asks, walking toward the garage where I notice a patch of newly tilled dirt. It looks like he is putting in ivy to climb up the north side of the garage to match the south side. He takes a dog treat out of his pocket. Howard rolls over before Dine throws it in the air for him to catch.

"Being thirteen? It is a piece of cake. Thanks for asking," I reply with a smile. "Is C.E. at home?" I watch him wipe the sweat from his brow with the handkerchief that he always carries. I think it is his most prized possession. Sometimes he sits and flattens the corners between his thumb and index finger, tracing the initials on it. He looks toward the treehouse.

As I walk away, I think I hear him say under his breath, "Just like her." But when I turn, he is almost to the garage.

"C.E.?" I call as I lean my bike up against the tree. I can see the tips of high-tops and know he is up there. I climb up and make enough noise so that I will not startle him in case he has been crying. Sometimes C.E. is emotional and does not want anyone to know he cries over things like dropping his buttered toast facedown, watching worms get eaten by a bird, or getting kicked in the pants by a girl.

When I reach the top, he is not crying; he is angry. I can tell because the tips of his ears are red. He is pulling the petals off some daisies from his garden. This is not a good sign. Before I ask if he wants to go to town with me, I sit and stare in the same direction as he does and wait for him to talk.

After ten minutes of silence and twenty bald daisies, I clear my throat. "Do you remember Christmas three years ago?" I ask but I do not wait for a reply; I start to giggle. "We were so bored while all the grown-ups played cards. My grandpa snuck us a package of Oreos and milk. Instead of eating them, we chewed four or five cookies and took turns playing dentist by picking out the cookies from the other's teeth with the end of a watercolor brush. We went downstairs to show our cookie-encrusted teeth when we ran into the mayor's mother bringing a gift for Sweet Betty Sue. You were so embarrassed, you fainted on the stairs." I start laughing so hard I accidentally pass gas.

"Oh, my golly, golly gosh!" I say, quite shocked. "Excuse me!" Then I roll over onto my side with yet another fit of giggles. I can tell he is laughing, even though he's trying hard to stay mad.

After another few minutes, he looks over at me and notices I am in my painting overalls. He lets out a sad laugh and shakes his head. "You got in trouble again." He sighs. "You want me to help you paint?"

I slug him on the shoulder. "I'll buy you a shake at Rexall's drugstore if you go into town with me." He grabs at his arm and winces. I immediately pull up his sleeve and see several bruises of different shades.

I stand up with my fists on my hips and yell, "Darn it, C.E. You have got to start sticking up for yourself. Those Bennett brothers will break you in half one of these days if you don't fight back!"

He turns and looks out the window of the treehouse. I think he is crying again. "They are so much bigger than me," he says with a quiet sniffle.

I can tell C.E. is wearing his homemade Superman T-shirt underneath his buttoned shirt. It makes him feel strong on his days when he is bullied. He jumps up and heads straight down the ladder. "Let's get into town," he says. "I could use a shake."

I decide not to say anything more about how he should stick up for himself. I do not like to see C.E. crying or upset. It darn near kills me.

We race our bikes to the paint store. As the bell rings when we open the door, Jeff and Denny Spazzecki are laughing at each other's jokes from behind the color counter. Jeff hammers a sign up on the wall while Denny holds the ladder. "Jeff, look who it is," Denny says.

"I didn't know a button could walk," Jeff says, wiping his hands on his apron before hitting Denny on the head. Denny smacks Jeff on the back, and they throw their heads back and laugh at their very unfunny joke.

Jeff walks up to us with three swatches of the color blue he grabs from the counter. "So what trouble are you in now, Missy Lou? Is it the barn, the kitchen, or the front porch this time?" He winks at Denny.

"Let's see, you've already painted the parlor, the store, and the foyer this year," Denny says, counting with his fingers. I roll my eyes at them, and C.E. cannot stop laughing. I hit the middle swatch. "Ah, it's the front porch and shutters, Jeff. Prepare the paint," he says with his fist in the air. "And you owe me two dollars. I told you it would be the shutters!"

Howard starts to bark as they all laugh at me. Jeff and Denny reach down to pet him. "I'm glad to see he is doing so well. Last year your grandpa asked for one of Mitzi's puppies. The day we dropped him off, it was raining like crazy. Well, you remember that day," Jeff says.

Denny knocks him over onto the floor and they both start to laugh. "He looks good and strong now, doesn't he?" he says and helps Jeff back up.

The Spazzecki brothers look exactly alike, except Jeff is fatter and Denny is uglier. But they are the nicest guys my grandpa ever worked with. As they start to arm-wrestle on the counter, I grab C.E.'s arm and walk to the door.

"Thanks, ladies," I say. "Don't hurt yourselves fighting over who gets to make dinner tonight." I hear them hoot and holler as we leave.

We walk next door to Rexall's and order our milkshakes. Between the Spazzecki and the milkshake, C.E. has forgotten about being bullied. I even let him eat the whipped cream and the cherry on top and the chunks of strawberries at the bottom. I laugh when he picks bits of berries out of his braces with the stem of his cherry.

While we wait, C.E. spins the magazine rack around in circles looking for a comic book to buy. I pull out some loose buttons, a fishing line, and a few beads from the button store and start stringing them together.

Charlie Hoon and Leonard Meadow are debating with C.E. about the newest comics. "No, no, no," Charlie says. "Picture this—The Flash with Superman's powers versus the Martian Manhunter with Batman's powers."

"Well, that isn't fair, though," C.E. says. "The Justice League would never fight or turn on one another."

Leonard hits the comic and interjects, "Wait. Remember when the Justice League was ..."

I roll my eyes at the boys at the comic rack and turn my attention back to my baubles and beads. I slurp the remainder of the milkshake loud enough to make C.E. turn around. I wave to Charlie and Leonard as they make their purchases at the counter. C.E. decides to buy the newest *Superboy and Tales of the Legion of Superheroes* comic, *Starfinger*, and a back issue from February's *Justice League of America*, Volume 33. He says goodbye to Charlie and Leonard and comes to sit at the soda counter. He looks down into the empty glass and pours the last of the ice cream into his mouth.

I finish tinkering with the collection of things from my pocket and realize I have made a bracelet.

"That's nice. Now let's go," he says and leaves a nickel and a dime at the counter for a tip. I put the bracelet in my pocket. I wonder if I could make and sell jewelry at the store to help bring in more customers and money. I will ask my Sweet Betty Sue sometime.

I carry the paint on my bike, and C.E. tries to read his comic while riding his own. I am relieved when we finally reach my house. While I paint the front door and the shutters, C.E. reads his comic books to me.

"The Alien-ator transforms the Justice League members into aliens!" C.E. says in shock. "This one is almost better than last December's comic featuring the criminal scientist Axel Storm."

He loves comic books and superheroes. His favorite is Superman. He is always so entertaining when he reads his comics aloud. I think he likes to get lost in the stories. Knowing that each story has a triumphant ending, bullies get what they deserve, and the hero saves the day gives C.E. comfort. What I think he especially likes about superheroes is that they have an alter ego. It gives him hope that he can be the ordinary person he is and maybe one of these days turn into a superhero. I think he loves Superman the most because his alter ego is a nerd with glasses.

Clark Kent is the only reason C.E. will wear his glasses. If only he'd get his hair cut. The problem is he's terrified of sharp objects, especially near his face.

C.E. hopes that one day he will no longer have to wear glasses, his gazillion million freckles will fade, and his hair won't look so much like a girl's, flowing beautifully with dark locks framing his sweet face.

We take a break from what we are doing and head into the kitchen. Dine is having lunch and talking to Sweet Betty Sue. She pours us a glass of iced tea and looks at me as I gulp it down.

"Hmm, this kitchen could use a good coat of that paint as well, don't you think, Missy Lou?" she says as she turns to the fridge. I am completely shocked. Howard has never gotten me into this much trouble before. I cannot figure out what he did to warrant this punishment.

"Well," I start to reply. "The kitchen looks great. You're too hard on yourself." She knows this is my way of questioning her punishment. I place the bracelet I made earlier at the drugstore on the table. Dine smiles and nods his approval at it before winking at me and taking a sip of his iced tea.

"My cuff is missing, and I think Howard took it the day he came into the parlor and broke my curio door," she says sadly. Now I know why I am in so much trouble.

A shirt cuff is not a big deal, but the one she is talking about means a great deal to her. This last year she has held on to that shirt cuff, and just this last week, she put it in a little box in her curio cabinet in the parlor. She will not tell me why it's so important or what shirt it's from.

When I first noticed the cuff, I asked her about it. She politely told me, "Please, just use your imagination. I can't talk about it now." I have not asked her about it since. But the look on her face now moves me to believe that this is the most precious item she owns in the world.

I sit sipping my iced tea, look up at Sweet Betty Sue, and smile. "I think the kitchen could use a coat of paint, now that I look around." The kitchen is baby blue and white everywhere. There is not a speck of any other color. Even the dishes and glasses are blue.

I look at C.E. and kick his foot. "I bet we could find that cuff easily. Are you up for the challenge, Detective?" I ask.

"Let's do it," he replies and grabs an apple. He stops at his dad's chair. "Oh, and it was nice to see you, Dad. I will be home late. Missy Lou and I are headed to Thimble Creek to try and catch fish later this afternoon, and then we're going to finish painting the front door."

"Yeah, we're going to use all the new lures in my new tackle box," I say and take a large bite out of C.E.'s apple.

Sweet Betty Sue takes her large wooden spoon from the pot on the stove and waves it at C.E. "You should go get a haircut instead of fishing, C.E," she teases. Dine nods at us and wipes his brow with his handkerchief.

We stop outside the swinging kitchen door so that I can tie my shoes. C.E. eats the apple quickly so I cannot take it from him again. His cheeks look like a chipmunk. I laugh and shake my head at him. "Remember last summer when we did detective work for Dandelion?"

C.E. laughs so hard that a snot bubble comes out of his nose. He chokes on his apple, so I slap him hard on the back until pieces of it hit the floor. He helps me clean them up.

We hear Dine clear his throat to speak through the kitchen door. We freeze on our hands and knees to listen. "You know, it might help the both of you if you talk about that cuff."

C.E.'s eyes are watering as he holds in his cough. I place my finger on my lips to shush him.

Dine continues, "It also might help if you talk about things with her instead of always making her paint any-time she or her dog does something wrong." He finishes his iced tea and heads for the back door before she can put him in his place.

Dine does all the handyman work at the house, the store, the barn, and the factory. My grandpa and he had served in World War II together. Dine has always spoken highly of my grandpa. I have seen Dine's eyes well up with tears when telling me stories about him. Maybe that's where

C.E. gets his sensitivity. The one thing I know for sure about Dine is that my grandpa was and still is the most respected person in his life. "Your grandpa had the most profound influence on me, and even though he's gone, his life still affects mine and all those who knew him."

I wish I had more stories about Grandpa. I wish I had asked more questions about his life while he was still around. I feel a weight on my shoulders. I think being a teenager is going to be harder than I originally thought. I am trying to find out who I am and who my mom was and find a few missing pieces to my grandpa's life. Maybe the first story to unlock is the one behind that shirt cuff.

Chapter Three

A boy doesn't have to go to war to be a hero; he can say he doesn't like pie when he sees there isn't enough to go around. —Edgar Watson Howe

I HEAR THE CLOCKS chime at noon below my room. It is the longest chime of the day, so it takes a minute for the reverberations of the clocks to settle after the twelfth chime. I like to place my face up against the wall and feel the vibrations tickle my cheek. As the last chime settles, I hear Howard scratching at my bedroom door.

Usually, he howls or barks when he wants to get in my room and the door is closed. His scratching lets me know that he has a secret message tied to his collar. It took C.E. and me two weeks to train Howard as our messenger in our detective work. We started using Howard when we realized the phone lines might be tapped.

We trained Howard to follow C.E.'s special whistle for a secret message and a reward. C.E. ties the detective note on Howard's collar and rewards him with a strip of bacon. Howard knows that I keep treats in my room just for him when he performs this task and is always eager to deliver the notes. So when the urgent scratching comes to my door, I know there is a detective message.

I feed Howard his treat and plop down on my bed to read the note. C.E.'s handwriting is flawless as well as his drawings of two detectives in suits, hats, sunglasses, and superhero capes.

Detective W.W.

(Wonder Woman, but you knew that),

Our mission today is to trace the steps of our furry culprit to find where the cuff is hidden. If you are ready for the mission, meet me at the you-know-what by the you-know-where, and bring you-know-who at you-know-when.

Destroy this message in two minutes, or it will self-destruct, and it won't be pretty.

Signed,

Detective S.M.

(Superman, you know, the man who can fly, stop bullets, etc.)

At 1:00 I take Howard to meet C.E. on the covered bridge over Thimble Creek. I have packed a lunch for us to eat while we look for clues to lead us to the missing cuff.

We sync our watches and go over the few hand gestures we made up when we formed the detective agency years ago: eyes forward, I am hungry, run, and high five. As we leave the bridge to follow Howard on his path toward the cuff, the Bennett brothers jump out from behind a bush and grab C.E. by the front of his shirt.

"Give us your money, punk puke!" the older brother yells. The younger brother points a sharp stick in my direction, threatening to jab me. Howard starts to growl and stands on his hind legs in front of me. They laugh when they see Howard trying to defend me.

"You need a little mutt as your bodyguard now?" the older brother says. He shakes C.E. harder, and C.E. fumbles to get his change out of his pants pocket.

C.E. gets his hand loose from his pocket and yells, "Here, just take it!" And then he throws the money in his face. The older Bennett brother shoves C.E. to the ground. C.E. cuts his lip on his braces on impact. The younger Bennett brother drops his stick when he sees the blood from C.E.'s mouth.

My heart races so fast that I can hear it in my head and feel it on the tips of my fingers and toes. I want to scream or move, but I am frozen in place, horrified at the sight of blood from C.E.'s mouth.

Howard is still growling. I pull his leash tight, so he won't attack but lose my grip, and Howard charges toward the younger Bennett brother, who picks up the stick again and strikes Howard on his front shoulder.

"No!" I scream, falling to the ground and trying to stop the bleeding with pressure from my hands. When the Bennett brothers see Howard laying limp on the ground and whimpering, they run away laughing and then yell, "Stupid dog!"

C.E. yanks the red bandana from my head and wraps Howard's shoulder. I start shaking with heavy sobs. C.E. picks Howard up and runs toward his house.

I turn and throw an apple from my lunch bag in the direction of the Bennett brothers. They turn and laugh again. I grab my bag and follow C.E. All I can see is dust. He is running faster than I have ever seen anyone run in my life.

By the time I get to the kitchen, C.E. has already wrapped Howard in a warm blanket, turned on the water tap, and placed a first aid kit on the counter. I carefully move Howard onto my lap. He whimpers. I try to control my shaking while I weep because it makes Howard cry even more.

"Missy Lou, get a hold of yourself. You're making Howard wince," C.E. calmly whispers as he turns the faucet to a slow trickle. The sound of running water calms Howard and surprisingly, me as well. He places a warm washcloth on Howard's wound, and Howard jumps in my arms. "Hold him still, but be gentle," C.E. says, his eyes focused on the wound.

He grabs a bottle of hydrogen peroxide and a gauze pad. He looks me in the face and nods to me. When I nod back, he removes the warm rag and places the gauze pad on the wound to sterilize it. Howard yelps, and I hold him down.

I try to calm the both of us by smoothing Howard's head, and before I realize what C.E. has done, Howard is asleep. His wound is clean and dressed. C.E. has also placed a warm water bottle under Howard's belly to make him comfortable. C.E. notices my breathing is shaky and starts to breathe in through his nose and out his mouth. I mimic him and soon am calm and feeling much better.

We sit in silence across the table from one another. Whenever I begin to choke up again, C.E. breathes in and out as before to keep me calm. I get so worked up when those I love hurt. The ache in my heart for Howard's pain is exactly like the hurt I felt when C.E. had a rock thrown at his head in the fifth grade. Someone threw a small rock at him while he was climbing on the jungle gym at school. Blood poured down his face and neck. I screamed and ran for the teacher. I helped carry him to the nurse's office and sat in the chair next to him gasping for air between my sobs. C.E. was calm and patted my hand as his wound was tended to. After his face was cleaned up, we saw only a small pin prick of a wound in his hairline. He did not even need a bandage. I made the nurse place one on his wound regardless.

When I saw Howard get stabbed, my heart throbbed again. I am amazed at C.E. and grateful for the way he saved Howard today. He is brave when he does not think about it too much. He completely ignored the fact that his mouth was bleeding and took charge of the situation. I look up and smile at him as he licks his lip and applies a warm rag to it.

I finally relax, though my eyes are dry but swollen. "C .E., you were so fast, and you knew exactly what to do for Howard. Thank you."

He looks up with an angry face that startles me. "I couldn't defend myself or you. All I could do was run away after the worst had happened," he says. He hits the table with his fist, and Howard stirs in my arms.

"Maybe I should lay Howard down on the couch," I suggest instead of acknowledging his outburst.

We walk into the front room, and C.E. gently places Howard on the soft recliner. We both sit on the couch opposite Howard and watch him sleep. I can tell C.E. is still upset but does not know what to say. I feared the Bennett brothers too, and I did not know how to defend myself either. I pat his hand, and he flinches while kicking his foot at the coffee table in front of him so hard that the bottom drawer knob falls off. I gasp. "C.E., I've never seen you so worked up," I say cautiously.

He drops to the floor to fix the drawer. He lets out a long, heavy sigh. "You've never been involved before," he says.

C.E. is right. In all the years that he has been bullied, I have never been there to witness it and have never been threatened personally until today.

When he pulls the drawer out to twist the knob back onto it, we find that it is full of old war pictures and letters postmarked from 1945. The picture on top is of my grandpa and Dine.

I'm not sure if we should be looking through the letters, but C.E. opens one and reads it quietly.

"These are amazing," C.E. says after finishing the letter. He reads more and passes each one to me to read. "They were close friends," he comments about the picture of the two soldiers standing side by side in front of an airplane.

We look around the room to make sure we are alone, and that Howard is still sleeping comfortably. "Read the next one," I say. He licks his swollen lip and reads a letter from my grandpa to his dad.

August 9, 1944
Dine:
I am relieved to hear that the wound to your leg did not warrant a trip to the hospital. All the same, take care of yourself and watch your back.

I just want you to know it takes a special kind of courage to do what you have done while in the face of adversity. Most would walk away, but I believe that if we see someone weaker than ourselves being mistreated and we have the strength and willpower, it is our responsibility to take action and do the right thing. When possible, avoid harm to another; but confront the problem and try to resolve it. Only after three attempts to make peace would I suggest using physical force.

It is not easy being a soldier. It is not easy to have courage every day. It is not easy to do the right thing when it may require the sacrifice of your own life. There is no sacrifice too great when what we do is for the good of mankind and our nation. Protect yourself, those you love, and those who need it. Above all, always stand for what you know is right.

Sincerely,
Sergeant Howard Button

Glider Base Camp, India Station
Bunker 24
*P.S. Say hello to Barty Stein. I hope he recovers quickly
from the flu.*

After three hours of reading letter after letter, C.E. and I place them back in the drawer and head to the kitchen for something to eat.

Reading those letters made both of us feel much better. I feel reconnected to my grandpa and have gained a better understanding of Dine's admiration for him.

After ten minutes of scrounging through the fridge, we resign ourselves to eating out of a tub of whipped cream with two spoons. Dine walks through the door and turns the radio down. After he washes his hands at the sink, he throws a pack of Bazooka gum on the table and places down a casserole before grabbing some plates and forks.

"Mrs. Davis is paying me in casseroles for the next week for the work I'm doing on her yard." He serves mounds of a noodle–like substance covered with green beans onto the three plates. "I assume you are staying for dinner too, Missy Lou?" he asks. I take a plate and start to eat.

I smile at him and say, "Thanks," through a mouthful of food.

C.E. starts to open the pack of bubble gum, but Dine clears his throat and says, "Not until you finish your din-ner, C.E."

"Fine." C.E. pouts.

"Thanks for the gum," I say.

Dine sits at the table and tucks a napkin into the neck of his shirt. "It's not from me. Crystal gave it to me while we waited in line at the market," he says. He eats his dinner, and C.E. and I stare at one another. We are not sure if we should tell Dine about our encounter with Crystal Bennett's sons this afternoon.

I open my mouth to tell him what happened to C.E. when Dine says, "Crystal said she knew you two loved gum and thought you might want a treat." He pauses to wipe his brow. "She sure is a fine lady, so prim and proper. One of the few sweet people who walk the earth."

He pauses again and then looks back at us as we roll our eyes. She is indeed an amazingly wonderful and talented woman, but we hate her boys. Dine pulls the newspaper from the counter behind him and glances at C.E.'s lip.

He slaps the paper open and adds, "It's a shame those boys of hers are such a menace. Their daddy was the same way as a young kid. He didn't stop bullying the kids at school until he got clocked in the jaw," Dine says. He turns the radio to the news.

Neither of us has anything to say. We both know what C.E. has to do to get those Bennett brothers to stop bullying him and the other kids at school, but C.E. isn't ready. I think Dine knows it too. I can tell by the concerned look on his face that he hopes for C.E.'s sake that he will take a stand soon.

Dine looks over his paper and sees the worry on C.E.'s face. "I'm not defending those boys," he says, "but if I had the names given to them at birth, I think I would also have some anger issues to work out. It doesn't help matters what their daddy did."

I pipe up angrily. "So because they have dumb names, it's OK for them to be bullies?"

Dine smiles at me tenderly. "No, not at all. But behind every bully's action is their pain. Sometimes, bullies are acting out what they have learned from their own experience of being bullied."

"So how is C.E. supposed to defend himself and stop getting bullied?" I demand.

Dine is smoothing his face with his palms. I can hear the scratching from his whiskers being pulled down. "Never despair," he says to C.E. He turns to me and says, "Only C.E. can be the one to make the change in himself." He pauses then looks at both of us. "You must think heroically to become heroic. Only you can save yourself."

He taps C.E.'s hand with his fork and says, "Now, stay out of that whipped cream."

We open the package of gum and start to shove as many pieces into our mouths as possible. Dine turns up the radio a little louder to listen to the news of the Vietnam War.

"President Johnson announced his order to increase the number of United States troops in South Vietnam from 75,000 to 125,000 and to double the drafted per month from 17,000 to 35,000," the anchor reports. We chew our gum rapidly to work enough spit into it to make a good-sized bubble as the news continues, "Four thousand paratroopers from the 101st Airborne Division have arrived in Vietnam, landing in Cam Ranh Bay."

C.E. and I try to see who can blow the largest bubble at the table and between the pop, pop of our bubbles, Dine strains to hear the news.

"We Americans know, although others appear to forget, the risk of spreading conflict. We still seek no wider war …" Pop. Pop. "We are not about to send American boys nine or ten thousand miles away from home to do what Asian boys ought to be doing for themselves." Then there is silence at the table. We stop blowing bubbles and look at Dine.

"We now bring to you President Johnson's address from the noontime conference yesterday from the White House. 'I do not find it easy to send the flower of our youth, our finest young men, into battle. I have spoken to you today of the divisions and the forces and the battalions and the units, but I know them all, everyone. I have seen them in a thousand streets, in a hundred towns, in every state in this union working and laughing and building and filled with hope and life. I think I know, too, how their mothers weep and how their families sorrow.' The U.S. bombing of North Vietnam resumes—" With a click, Dine turns off the radio and folds his newspaper.

C.E. swallows hard. His face is pale.

"You're only turning fourteen in October, Son. It's 1965. If you were to be drafted, the war would have to still be in full force by the year 1969 when you turn eighteen. I do not see this carrying on longer than the end of the year. No more American boys will make it over to Vietnam," he says, trying to reassure C.E. that his worst nightmare will not come true. He pauses, and a great sadness takes him over. "No young boy should ever have to go to war."

He reopens his newspaper and hides his face behind it. C.E. watches the back of the newspaper for movement. I lean over to C.E. and elbow him. "Let's go read some of your old comics before I have to go home. You told me there was a cool issue with Wonder Woman in it." C.E. seems relieved to change the subject and leave the kitchen.

As we head upstairs, C.E. comments, "There should be superheroes in wars. We'd win for sure."

I think I hear Dine faintly say, "There are superheroes in war."

Up in C.E.'s room, he reads one of his comics, using the appropriate high and low voices for Wonder Woman and the Flash. He jumps off his bed and grabs another comic book. "If the Flash, combined with Batman's superpowers and the Martian Manhunter's abilities, was in the war right now, it would be over. If the enemies are as bad as when Owlman zapped Green Lantern with his Illumina-Gun, only Superman alone could end the war." He reverently places each comic in a protective cover and then into a box which he lays in his desk drawer.

I offer to split the last piece of gum with him, but he does not take it. "I'm full," he says, touching my hand and smiling at me.

"Thanks. I'll practice blowing the world's largest bubble and show you tomorrow," I say, slugging his arm before I leave for home.

Howard is waiting by the door for me. He tries to look brave by standing on all four legs, but I can tell his wound is still hurting. I pick him up and carry him in my arms.

I walk down the path and see Dine working in his greenhouse. He meets me at the gate while cleaning his hands with a rag.

"You want me to drive you and Howard home?" he asks.

I shake my head. "Thanks, though. We'll be OK." I look back toward his greenhouse. "Your daisies look great this year."

Dine nods his thanks and opens the gate for me.

I think that growing daisies is first a hobby for him, but he also sells them to the corner market and the drugstore. He helps people all over the town with their landscaping and usually gets paid in casseroles, quilts, or canned peaches. He is the gentlest man I know.

I can see the front porch light glowing through the trees down the lane from the button factory. I can almost smell my grandpa's pipe, and I remember him sitting on the front porch on the rocking chair. I think back on a long day and am glad C.E. and I read those letters from my grandpa to Dine.

I make my way up to the steps and turn to see Venus shining brightly in the night sky. I cross my fingers and whisper, "I wish C.E. will be the hero I know he is deep down inside." Howard gives a little bark as if to say, "I hope he dreams he's Superman tonight, too."

When I enter the kitchen, I smell angel food cake. It is not Sunday, the usual day for it. I place Howard down on a chair and help my Sweet Betty Sue with the dishes. She passes me a plate. "Is there any cake left?" I casually ask.

"What cake? There isn't any cake," she says.

"It smells like angel food cake. Is it just my imagination?"

She clears her throat and looks away from the sink. "I guess it must be your imagination." She dries her hands on a towel while smoothing her apron and walks from the kitchen.

I finish cleaning the dishes, dry them, and put them away. While I am in the cupboards, I look for cake but cannot find one anywhere. I pick Howard back up from the chair and carry him up to my room. My stomach growls. I am craving cake!

Chapter Four

Aspire rather to be a hero than merely appear one.
—Baltasar Gracian

THE NEXT DAY, I come downstairs to the smell of angel food cake again. The clocks chime twelve when I walk into the kitchen for lunch. I cannot wait to have a piece of cake. I swing the door open and see a tuna sandwich on the table with a tall glass of milk.

I sit down and eat as fast as I can, knowing that C.E. will be here soon to go fishing with me at the creek. I finish my milk as Sweet Betty Sue walks into the kitchen.

"Where's the cake?" I ask.

She touches the sides of her hair as if making sure her head is still on her shoulders and shrugs. "There's no cake, Missy Lou."

"But I just checked the oven and it's still hot. And there's a cake pan in the sink!"

She grabs her broom and sweeps around my feet. I quickly lift them. "I hear a customer. I think it might be Mrs. Parker or Crystal. They both have special orders to be picked up today," she says and swats my backside with the broom while I make my way from the kitchen.

"But the cake?" I plead.

"There's no cake," she says and laughs.

I walk through the doorway to the store and find Crystal Bennett waiting at the counter. I know what her order is going to be today. Something pink, sweet, and beautiful for her daughter, Lizzie. I love Crystal but loathe her bully sons. I especially cannot stand her snobby daughter.

I meet her pretty face, and I melt. With everything I have against her children, I cannot help but adore Crystal. She dyes her hair blond (I can tell from the inch of black roots at her scalp), and she wears so much makeup. I cannot tell if she is trying to hide her face or accentuate it. Either way, I still think she is pretty. She wears thick-rimmed glasses and has the most glamorous smile, which warms me every time I see her. When she laughs, it sounds more like a flirt, regardless of the company that she is laughing with. Today she is wearing a white poplin drop waist dress. Her hair is tied back with a cream scarf, and the delicate earrings hanging from her ears nearly kiss her shoulders. She is a breath of fresh air on such a hot summer day.

If I were to choose who I could be when I am older, it would be Crystal. She is the definition of elegance. She always carries two or three novels in her bag. One is always Jane Austen's Pride and Prejudice. Of course, her daughter Lizzie is named after her favorite character.

I sigh as I see her at the counter. Everything she does seems like a lovely dance, even the movement of placing her bag on the counter or clasping her shawl closed.

When she sees me walk in, she glides over to me and hugs me softly. She takes my face in her hands, like she always does, and looks deep into my eyes. "Thirteen years old. Happy belated birthday, Missy Lou." She hugs me one more time and takes my hand to guide me to the counter.

"Is my special order in, Missy?" she asks. She opens her bag and pulls out a fan. While she timidly fans her face, I stoop down under the register and look under her name for any special order. In a small brown bag, I find three sheets of beautifully carved pink pearl buttons in the shape of roses. A part of me wants to scream because I know these are going on an undeserved dress for Lizzie.

I smooth the bag and slide it over to her. She pats my hand sweetly. "Here are three skeins of yarn for Betty. We agreed to an exchange," she says, placing the red, blue, and yellow skeins of yarn on the counter.

I cannot get the bitterness out of my mouth when I think of Lizzie. I want to tell Crystal what her sons did to Howard, C.E., and myself the other day on the bridge. I nearly have the nerve built up, but she cries at the sight of the beautiful buttons. I decide not to say a word.

She takes my hand and helps me out from behind the counter to hug me one last time. "Thank Betty for the beautiful choice in buttons. Lizzie's dress for the festival will be stunning."

I nod my head and force a smile that is so tight I can feel my braces poking the inside of my lips.

She stops and turns at the door. "I'll see you at the dance?" she asks.

"You bet," I say through my anger. I swing my arms front and back and clasp them in front of me as I watch Crystal back out of our driveway.

There is a pain mounting in my chest as I watch her car get smaller and smaller in the distance. My thoughts creep from my head out my mouth. I try to stop them, but it's no use. The tears stream down my face. Through clenched teeth and blurry eyes, my anger seeps.

"Lizzie Bennett doesn't deserve Crystal as her mom. She does not deserve a pretty dress. And she does not deserve those stupid rose buttons! Crystal should be my mom. My mom should not have died. I try to be a good girl. I try. But I will never have a mom," I cry in a gritted whisper.

I watch the dust settle on the driveway. When I see that there is no one around, I run out of the house. I run, and I run, and I run. Tears sting my eyes. My heart feels like it is tearing in half, but slowly, torturing me as I sink deeper into my bitterness toward Lizzie.

I stop underneath the covered bridge not because I am tired of running, but because my chest and heart feel like they are ready to burst into flames.

I feel myself drifting off to sleep as I lie at the edge of the water but am startled awake when my chest feels like it is hit with a baseball bat.

I make myself breathe in through my nose and out through my mouth like C.E. taught me. I look at my watch. Two o'clock. C.E. is probably waiting at the house to go fishing. I grab the nearest rock and throw it into the creek.

My heart is still pounding like a caged lion that is trying to escape.

I throw more rocks into the creek until I calm down enough to go back home. Halfway there, I see Howard hobbling down the road to meet me. I kneel and catch him in my arms. He licks my face and wags his tail. I nuzzle into his neck. "I love you, Doggy," I whisper.

I pick him up and carry him back home with me and devise a plan for the next prank I will pull on Lizzie. I tell Howard all the great tricks that I have pulled on Lizzie and laugh. "I've already ruined her most beloved doll, cut a hole in her science fair project, tied her shoelaces together in track, and ...." I trail off. My stomach lurches. There are countless pranks I have pulled on Lizzie. I could fill a notebook.

Behind every bully's actions is their pain, I hear Dine's voice in my head. "My pain," I say to myself.

I realize that I have bullied Lizzie. Maybe it is because of the loss of my mother. Since we were five years old there has only been friction between us. I have held a grudge against her for having a mother all these years. It still does not explain why she has held a grudge against me and has pulled her pranks on me year after year.

It seems that this year she is trying to keep the rivalry alive by outshining me in everything. She has already made the drill team, tried out for girls' basketball, and earned a solo at the Town Festival. Something inside me now wants the conflict between us to end. Now that I realize what I have done and why I've done it, I just want to ignore her and be ignored. I do not want to become friends or anything, just not enemies. "Can you imagine, Howard? Lizzie and me friends!"

Howard is asleep in my arms when I enter the house. I quietly close the front door behind me.

"Missy Lou," Sweet Betty Sue calls from her parlor. "Have you found my cuff?" she asks when I reach the doorway.

I put Howard down on the floor next to my feet and take a seat across from Sweet Betty Sue. "No, I'm sorry. I'll talk to C.E. again about it today." I see the three skeins of yarn from Crystal and realize what this means.

"Stick out your arms, dear," she says. Sweet Betty Sue wraps pounds of yarn around my wrists while she rolls it into a ball for knitting something later.

I sit in the parlor sucking on the same three lemon drops for an hour. Sweet Betty Sue goes to the kitchen on three separate occasions.

"It smells like—" I am about to say cake, but the look on her face dares me to say it, and I end my sentence with a short whistle instead.

She smiles at me and continues to roll the yarn into a ball. "Did Crystal like the buttons?" she asks.

She finishes rolling the last bit of yarn. I nod and stretch my arms up in the air. "She hugged me three times. That is always a good sign. I hope Lizzie likes her dress for the dance," I say the last part with a little bitterness by accident. Just an hour ago I decided to let it go, but I guess I still need a little time. I smile and let out a nervous giggle, hoping she did not notice I mentioned Lizzie.

Sweet Betty Sue looks up from her yarn and pushes her glasses up her nose. "Were you planning on going to the dance?" she asks with genuine surprise.

We have not talked about it until now, and I am not planning on going. I have told everyone I would not miss it, but that is just to be polite. Going to the dance is another thing altogether.

I do not own a single dress, and this is the first year I am old enough to attend the dance. It would be dumb to show up in overalls or my blue jeans. I have been so busy painting everything baby blue because of all the mischief Howard has been into lately that I have not gathered up the courage to ask Sweet Betty Sue to make me a dress for the dance.

I am not sure I want to go. I try to change the subject. "Howard's feeling much better," I say.

She asks me again with a serious look on her face, "Are you going to the dance?"

I am so anxious to leave the room, grab my tackle box, and head down to the creek with C.E. that I blurt out the first thing to come into my head. "Of course, I'm going to the dance. What girl in town would not want to go? It's my first dance, and everyone who's anyone will be there."

I immediately realize I sound just like a snob. Sweet Betty Sue's mouth drops open and I run from the room before she can say anything to me about my attitude.

The truth is, I do not know how to dance. The only person I have ever danced with was my grandpa, and it was always while standing on his feet or accidentally stepping on them. I haven't worn a dress since the second grade when I was Goldilocks in the school play, and I don't think my Sweet Betty Sue will make me one as pretty as the one Lizzie is going to wear with those pretty rose buttons.

The only buttons I would want on my dress are the pearl ones I sneak into the shop to look at every other day when Sweet Betty Sue is not paying attention.

I hear my Sweet Betty Sue walk to the phone in the kitchen. I do not want to go through the kitchen to get my fishing pole, so I head for the front door. I stop in the hall when I hear her speak into the phone. "Crystal, how do you like your buttons?" I turn around to eavesdrop when Ms. Tovah Stein throws the front door open.

"Missy!" she exclaims. "I am missing two of the buttons I ordered. I think when I picked them up from you the other day, I might have dropped them." She frantically runs into the store to look for the buttons on the floor.

I follow her and go straight to the dustbin and broom. "I was supposed to finish sweeping and didn't. Maybe the buttons are in here," I say as I pour the dirt out of the bin. We both start spreading it out over the floor.

"Aha! There they are!" she says. "You clever girl, Missy."

I sweep up the dust again and dump it in the trash while Ms. Tovah Stein cleans the buttons with the velvet cloth we keep at the register.

She hugs me tightly and drags me with her to the front door. My face squishes into her side, and I start laughing. I have grown fond of the way she always hugs and drags me around. I feel she is the aunt I always wanted.

I walk her to the car and shut her door for her. She starts her engine, and the music from the radio blares so loud that it makes me jump. She puts her sunglasses on and looks toward the back of the house. She smiles when she sees C.E. He looks like he is talking to himself.

She leans one large arm out the window and pulls me close to her. "What are you wearing to the dance?" she asks.

I roll my eyes and shove my hands into my pockets. "If I go, most likely my overalls," I say quietly.

She takes her thin silver bracelet off her wrist and puts it on mine. There is a small-heeled silver slipper charm hanging on it. "As your fairy godmother, I demand that you have a little hope. The dance is not tonight. There's still time to get you ready for the ball," she says.

"Thanks," I say and look at the charm on the bracelet while she drives away. She honks as she leaves the property.

Ms. Tovah Stein is the most interesting person I know. She is always kind to me and tells me stories of all her travels and interesting people she has met. But for all her travels, she always says, "Ogdenville is where my home is and will be forever. All you need in life is in Ogdenville." She sounds like my grandpa when he used to talk about

Ogdenville. I cannot wait to see her perform at the Town Festival.

I head out back where C.E. is helping his dad fix the fence that borders our property and the mayor's mother's horse property.

"Hi, Dine," I say as I approach them at the fence. Dine tips his hat and winks as he heads off to the barn without saying anything to me. I can tell he knows something because his shoulders start to shake as he laughs.

When I reach C.E., he is kicking dirt up with his foot and looks a bit bashful. I cannot seem to make eye contact with him. He avoids looking at me, and it makes me mad. I put my hands on my waist and am ready to scold him when he lifts his head and looks at me.

"Want to go to the dance with me?" C.E. blurts out. Then, just as fast as he blurted out the question, he turns and runs from me, heading toward the fence. In his attempt to hurdle the fence, his shoe gets caught on a barb. He hangs from the fence by his tangled shoestrings.

I start laughing. The last time this happened was when we snuck into the mayor's mother's cow field and tied pink ribbons on the cows' tales for Valentine's Day two years ago. As he hung from the fence that time, a cow sauntered over and started to chew on his hair.

I know he is not hurt. I am not even laughing at his accident but rather that he asked me to the dance.

"It's not funny," he says as his face starts to turn red. "I'm serious." He looks around and swats at his head.

"There aren't any cows in the field today are there?" he asks, looking a little faint despite his face being red.

He knows I am not laughing at him on the fence. That is how well we know each other. I help him off the fence and even tie his shoes and dust his clothes off.

With our hands in our pockets and heads down, we kick the dirt on the path back to the house.

"I'll go with you," I answer and slug him on the arm. "Thanks for asking me." We smile at each other.

He slugs me back and yells, "Race you to the house!" And I eat his dust as I try to catch up.

When we reach the kitchen, I smell angel food cake again. The room is warm, but again, there is no cake in sight. We help ourselves to the ginger snaps on the table and talk about starting school in a few weeks.

C.E. gets up to wash his hands, and his belt gets caught on the tablecloth. The cloth and everything else on the table tumble down on top of C.E. who lies facedown on the floor.

After I stop laughing, we clean up the mess. He shakes the tablecloth out and pretends to use it as a large napkin. "This reminds me. What are you going to wear to the dance?"

"Good question. Let's think about it while we fish," I say, trying to change the subject and get out of the house.

He wraps the tablecloth around me and places a tea cozy on my head. "We should think of ways to earn some money so we can buy a dress down at the consignment store," he says seriously.

I open a pack of Double Bubble bubblegum, and we load four pieces each in our mouths.

"What about the attic?" C.E. suggests as he pulls the gum from his braces and wipes the slobber off his chin. "I bet there are loads of dresses and other stuff up there we can put together for you to wear," he says as he heads for the stairs.

"Why didn't I think of that?" I accidentally spit on him when I talk because of all the gum in my mouth. "Sorry," I squeak.

C.E. starts up the stairs, and I follow at his heels. I have not been in the attic since I was barely able to walk. I do not remember anything but a small round window that reminds me of a button. I hope we find a dress.

When we reach the third-floor landing, we find that the door is locked.

C.E. tries to open the door with his pocketknife just as I blow the world's largest bubble. I tap his shoulder to show him, but I frighten him, and he jumps back into my bubble which has reached the size of my head. Pop!

"Oh, my golly, golly gosh, C.E.!" I say frantically and start to laugh as I pick gum out of my eyebrows.

"Missy!" he cries and runs down to the bathroom while pulling gum from his hair.

I try for a whole ten minutes to get that Double Bubble out of his hair. "I wonder where the key to the attic is?" I say.

"How can you be thinking about that right now?" he asks. His reflection in the mirror becomes so pale that I think his freckles just might fade away as he has always wished. "Gum! There is gum everywhere!" he wails.

I sit him down on the toilet and grab the scissors from the medicine cabinet. "This is the only way," I say seriously. I think he might faint when I bring the scissors closer to his face. No wonder his hair is long and shaggy, no one can ever get close enough with the scissors. The last time he had his hair cut, Dine buzzed his whole head. The hair on his head now is two years' worth of growth, and it is covered in bright pink gum.

He shakes his head violently as I come closer.

"Cornelius Everblot Zog," I say slowly and steadily, which gets his attention. He hates his name. When I use it, he knows that I mean business. I hear him gulp, and he closes his eyes.

After twenty minutes of *snip, snip,* "Oops! Sorry," snip, it is done. The sink is full of beautiful black ringlets covered in pink Double Bubble. What a sight to see.

C.E. sighs in relief as he looks in the mirror. The color is back in his face. I think I see him stand a little taller too. "I feel different," he says as he looks right, then left, in the mirror. I haven't seen C.E.'s entire face in over a year. I had forgotten how vibrant blue his eyes are. Even behind his glasses, they seem to sparkle.

"You look different, too," I reply as if the wind has been knocked out of me. My cheeks burn a little.

He gathers up the hair and tosses it in the trash. "Thanks for the haircut," he says and slugs me on the arm, which hurts this time. My feelings are hurt that he slugged me, but I also would have been mad if he had not slugged me. *What is going on with me?* I feel mixed up in the head. Who knew a haircut could be so life-altering.

I walk him to the door. I do not feel like fishing anymore, so I don't bring it up again as he leaves the house. He walks past me as I hold the screen door open. He pauses and picks a wad of gum off my top lip and the tip of my nose. "Your face is still covered in gum." He laughs. "I'll think of some other way to get you a dress for the dance," he says as he puts his hands in his pockets.

"Thanks. I'll think of a plan too. Oh, and we still need to find that cuff. Sweet Betty Sue asked me about it again today," I say. Then I remember my face is covered in gum, and I slam the screen door shut. "Bye," I call out. He turns and slicks back his hair before waving to me.

I grab at my face and feel the sticky pink gum all over. I smile as I watch him walk home. I lean against the door and sigh.

I finish cleaning the bathroom as well as my face. I look down and find one last lock of hair with a big chunk of pink gum on it. It makes me smile. I walk into my room with it and place it in my jar of buttons and baubles.

I saw C.E. differently today. It half scares me, half excites me. C.E. saw himself differently too. He saw Superman's alter ego, Clark Kent, looking back at him.

I always saw Superman in C.E., but it is never the same until you start seeing it for yourself. I'm glad to see this small change in him. C.E. is on his way to finding out who he is. I wish I could say the same for myself. The only thing I have learned is that I've been a bully to Lizzie for years and didn't realize it, and now I have a funny feeling in my stomach every time I think about C.E. Maybe C.E. is right about people who are in love having rocks in their head, but right now I feel like I have rocks in my stomach.

Chapter Five

A hero is no braver than an ordinary man, but he is braver five minutes longer. —Ralph Waldo Emerson

Detective W. W.,

Found key. Asked my dad. It was on his key ring. No questions were asked. Was given the "What are you up to?" look. Entering potentially dangerous territory. Bring backup excuse for protection. Self-explosive letter. Terminate in the toilet for assurance.

Detective S.M.

(Superman. That's me, the one and only, remember?)

I read the letter that Howard delivered to me this morning. C.E. meets me on the top floor, and I feel apprehensive about going in. With my first step inside, my thoughts wander to my mother, and I wonder if there are things of hers up here.

"I don't even want to go to the dance anymore. Let's go look for the cuff instead," I plead. C.E. is more curious and aggressive than I am, and he pulls me into the room.

He pulls down a large box that once had Mildred written on it, but it was scratched out and replaced with the name Darla, which was scratched out and replaced with the name Harriet. He opens it and starts throwing old bonnets, gloves, and purses at me to try on.

"C.E., these are ancient. I cannot wear any of these. Besides, they smell like mothballs," I say as I try on a lavender shawl, black gloves, and pink bonnet. "If you like them so much, why don't you wear them?"

He shrugs and says, "All right." He puts on a black beaded hat and pulls the accompanying veil down over his face. He grabs the yellow parasol, opens it, and twirls it over his shoulder. I start to laugh, and he covers my mouth. I nod, remembering that I might get in trouble if I'm found up here.

C.E. puts on a pair of gloves and finds a purse that matches. He tips his hat and starts to say something when we hear a creak from the door. We freeze and look around to see if we have been caught. The floor makes a cracking noise, and we jump into each other's arms, dressed as old ladies when Howard jumps up on us. C.E. squeals. Howard knocks him to the ground and starts licking his face. C.E. looks as if he has seen a ghost.

I try to keep myself from laughing. I grab my stomach and cover my mouth and roll to the floor to try to suppress the giggles. C.E. takes off his accessories and grabs my shawl. He throws everything in the box and puts it away.

I shake my head at C.E. as I stop giggling and wipe the tears from my eyes. He slugs me on the arm and helps me up off the floor. We both follow Howard to a door across the room.

It's locked. C.E. pulls out the key to the attic and tries it in the lock. There is a soft click. C.E. turns the knob and slowly opens the door.

The first thing I notice when we walk inside is the matching round window on each of the opposing walls. The room must have been added to the factory much later, and from the contents it holds, it is meant to guard the most valuable of items.

I am amazed at how clean and dusted everything is. No drapes are covering any of the furniture, which is smooth and polished. The glass is clean, and everything is organized.

C.E. walks straight to the large shadow box hanging on the wall that encases my grandpa's war uniform, fully decorated along with a ceremoniously folded American flag. In the shadow box next to it are his goggles and gloves and a picture of him dressed and standing at attention in front of his plane.

The wall around his uniform holds war plaques, Medals of Honor, pictures with the president, and framed newspaper clippings. In the corner, there is a glass cabinet that holds all his guns.

It is quiet. I can hear the rhythm of my heartbeat in my head. The room is still, almost reverent. I am seeing my grandpa in his true form, a hero. He has always been a hero to me, but here is proof of his heroism toward his country and his troops. He looks so strong, determined, and full of life in the pictures.

The last year before he left me, he was very sick from cancer. I knew he was in pain, more pain than one person should ever experience in a lifetime. It was hard for me to watch. I felt as helpless as a mothball in a coffee mug. He never let anyone know how sick he was, how much pain he suffered, or the sadness he felt knowing that he was going to be leaving the place he loved so much, Sweet Betty Sue's side.

The day I knew he was not going to get better was the day he couldn't paint anymore. He had been a painter all his life. He painted houses with his dad and continued to paint nearly every building in our town. Everyone in town has had at least one bedroom, house, business, barn, or fence painted by my grandpa.

When he could not hold a paintbrush, I started painting for him. I took on all his jobs. He followed me to the work sites and would coach me on how to dip the paint, stroke the brush, and gain the patience needed to do a good job.

I was not with him when he died. He had a surge of energy and went to town with Sweet Betty Sue for a can of paint for a job I was going to do later that afternoon. He put on his favorite painting shirt and left the house with a smile.

I hugged him and told him I loved him. He pulled on my red bandana and smiled.

"Everything I love is right here in Ogdenville. Who could ask for more? What a blessed life," he said.

I waved goodbye from the porch. I got a call from the hospital two hours later saying that he had died.

I touch the two pocket watches that his grandparents brought over to America with them from Switzerland. How many times I asked him to tell me the story, I cannot recall. Seeing them makes me feel closer to him.

"Grandpa, tell me again," I would plead as a little girl. Slowly he would puff on his pipe, and after a moment, he would nod his head. I knew this meant I could climb up on his lap and he would tell me the story.

"Leslie and Mathilda had three hours before they would leave on the boat that sailed for America. They knew they would never see their beloved homeland again. They sold everything they owned other than a few items that fit in their trunk, to pay for passage to America. With a few extra dollars between them, they decided they would each purchase a reminder of their homeland for the other. They each showed up at the boat with a pocket watch for the other. This began the collection of watches and clocks that would continue down through the generations. That is why there are so many clocks in the house," he would say just in time for the chimes from all seventy-three clocks to ring.

As I remember the story, the clocks ring noon downstairs. I only have another thirty minutes before lunch and the call from my Sweet Betty Sue to wash up.

I survey the rest of the room. I follow a sunbeam from the window down to a chest of beautiful dark wood. On the front are carved roses, which are painted red. I know I'm not ready to open it, but I know I have found the answers to my past. I have found my mother's hope chest.

"Missy," C.E. whispers. I break my concentration from the chest and walk over to C.E. "Howard keeps sniffing at the drawer at the bottom of this dresser. Should we open it?" he asks. Everything else has been on display, so I have not felt like we have been doing anything wrong. Opening the drawer makes me feel like I am trespassing.

I get on my knees and pull very slowly. C.E. crouches over me to see what is inside. Howard seems to be holding his breath. Inside are three soft brown leather books titled *The Life I've Accomplished, The Events I Regret,* and *My Most Treasured Memories.*

C.E. gasps when he sees that the bottom of the drawer is filled with Superman comics.

"Do you mind if I just look carefully?" he pleads. I think I nod because he starts to read them while I continue to stare at the books, deciding which to read first.

I pick up The Events I Regret and start at the beginning, but I am surprised when I see there is only one page of entries. It makes me feel good to know my grandpa did not have that many regrets in his lifetime.

May 12, 1917. I forgot to send my mama a letter to reach her in time for Mother's Day. I feel just awful. I will make it up to her by purchasing a tablecloth while I am in Versailles once my troop gets their orders to France.

November 4, 1943. I only told Betty Sue "I love you" 99 times, even though I swore I would tell her 100 times before the boat sailed away.

June 22, 1944. I jumped on a mother and her baby to shield them from incoming gunfire, but the bullets pierced through me and straight into them, killing both before I could return them home.

January 2, 1945. I couldn't run fast enough to the medical tent to save that little girl. She died in my arms unnecessarily. If only I had run faster.

August 27, 1953. I wish I had hugged my son when his wife died instead of patting him on the back. I should have told him what I loved about her while she was living.

September 2, 1964. I should have told Missy Lou how much she looks like her mother when she wears that red bandana in her hair.

When I read the last entry, dated two days before my grandpa died, I break into sobs that feel so painful that it is as if I'm losing my grandpa all over again.

C.E. stops reading his comics and puts his arm around me. He reads the last entry and takes in a deep breath, letting it out slowly to help me calm down.

We sit on the floor a little longer while I gather my thoughts and wipe my face clean.

"Thanks, C.E.," I say as I run my nose across my sleeve.

"Anytime. Should we go fishing?"

"How about a game of checkers in the tree house? Best out of a hundred," I say.

He stands up. "It's a deal. Maybe we can have some of the cake I smell baking down in the kitchen."

I shake my head. "I smell it too, but there isn't any cake. We should be investigating this cake issue as well as that cuff," I say as he takes my hand. Howard doesn't move. He is asleep in my lap. "Maybe we better let him nap."

"I'll clean up, and then we can go," C.E. says, placing the comics back in the drawer. I cannot get Howard to wake up. I can tell his wound is still hurting because he takes more naps than he used to, and he always whimpers in his sleep now.

"We should let him sleep a little longer," C.E. says as he sits next to me. He pats Howard on the head and says, "Tell me about how you got Howard again. I like that story."

I smile down at my golden dog and tell his story.

"It was the afternoon of my grandpa's funeral. The rain came down in unrelenting sheets. No one was able to attend the services or the graveside memorial. Everyone had to go home. My Sweet Betty Sue and I felt that we were not able to properly mourn our loss or celebrate his life. When we got home, we stood at the back door and watched the rain pour down onto the garden. We were in a trance. It was raining so hard the tomatoes fell right off their plants. The noise from the rain was deafening.

"The day started dark and gloomy and by evening, it was still the same. It was strange to have such bad weather in September, but Sweet Betty Sue and I felt it was appropriate, considering our loss.

"Through the loud noise of the relentless rain, I kept telling Sweet Betty Sue that I heard a whimper outside.

'Drink your Postum. You'll feel better. I'm sure it's just the rain pounding down on the old tractor or something else out there,' she said.

"I thought for a moment I was hearing my sadness in my head as a faint cry. But after walking back to the screen door, I heard a distinct animal whimper.

"Sweet Betty Sue rolled her eyes at me and said, 'Take the umbrella. There's no use convincing you there's nothing out there.' She grabbed the umbrella from the closet.

"I went out. Halfway to the garage, I saw a small gold mound moving ever so slightly underneath the geraniums. I ran to it and scooped it up into my hands. It was so small, wet, and dirty.

"I took it inside and cleaned it in the kitchen sink. It was then that I realized it was a puppy. It was only a few days old and not ready to open its eyes yet. It was a cocker spaniel, I could tell. My grandpa had one as a young boy, and he had told me all about the dog and its breed.

"I pleaded with my Sweet Betty Sue to keep it and she said that whatever trouble the dog got into; I would receive the punishment. The dog was my responsibility.

"I told her I named him 'Howard.' She stopped in the middle of putting away the dishes and looked at me with pleading eyes. I told her, 'It's the only name for this dog on this day.'

"She told me not to expect her to love it or even like having it around. Then the rain stopped, and the moon glowed in the sky. I took him to bed with me, and he's been sleeping there ever since."

I watch Howard's ears perk up as I finish his story, "And that's the story of Howard, my most beloved dog, named after my most beloved grandpa."

C.E. smiles at me. "Great story. I never get tired of hearing it." He takes a deep breath. "Still up for a checkers tournament?" he asks.

We make sure the attic looks the same as when we found it and quietly close the door. There is a soft click as C.E. locks it.

I feel connected to my grandpa again. I realize he did not leave me. He has always been here, inside my memories. I may have lost my grandpa but not the relationship that I had with him. Our love for each other carries on. I feel less alone than I have in a year.

It is also a comfort knowing where the answers are about my mom when the time comes that I am ready for them.

We walk to the parlor to tell my Sweet Betty Sue we are having lunch in the tree house, but we stop when we hear Dine talking. We listen through the parlor door.

"They have the key to the attic," Dine tells her simply. I hear glass shatter on the floor and then a shuffle. "Now, now, Betty. What's done is done. Who knows what they got into or if they even went up yet?" Dine says, trying to smooth it over. I hear my Sweet Betty Sue sit back down in her chair and start clicking her knitting needles again.

"Don't look at me that way. You know how I am. I cannot face things the way you can. I am not ready to relive it all. The past is hard for me," she explains. "I miss him so much."

Dine shifts his weight, and I imagine that he is wiping his forehead. "Well, Betty, I think it's unfair that Missy Lou doesn't know her past. She needs to stay connected to her grandpa. You need to help her. All she has is you now," he says gently. We hear footsteps coming toward the door.

Before we can get caught, we run into the kitchen. I scribble a note that we are at the tree house, and we head out the back door. Howard thinks it is a game and chases us all the way, sore leg and all.

C.E. realizes that he is still holding onto a comic from the attic. I tell him he can keep it. He slips it into a protective cover and places it on his chest reverently. He then grabs the checkers and his notepad to keep score.

While I wait for C.E. to set up the game, I daydream about my grandpa. He is saving the mother and child and running as fast as Superman to save that little girl.

I want to be like my grandpa. I want to live with only a sheet of regrets and two whole books full of accomplishments and memories.

Chapter Six

We can't all be heroes because somebody has to sit on the curb and clap as they go by. —Will Rogers

I HAVE BEEN IN my bed all day. Not even the curious smell of angel food cake can get me to leave my room. I do not want to lift my head off the pillow. Howard plays with my feet as I move them back and forth under the covers. I stare at the ceiling and watch the propellers spin on the model plane. There is a scratching noise from outside my window. It is C.E. climbing up the honeysuckle vine to get into my room.

When he reaches my window, he swings one leg over and leans into the window frame. "Missy Lou, come on out. I'll let you have the big worms for fishing," he pleads, gasping for air. When I do not move or blink, he opens a comic that was secured to the inside of his shirt. "Fine. I'll just sit in your window and tell you about your grandpa's comic that you let me keep."

I still do not say anything. Howard walks in circles on my bed and then lies down, perks his head up, and stares at C.E., waiting to be told a story. At least he is enthusiastic.

"This is *Action Comic* No. 1 from June of 1938! Amazing." C.E. reads it to me. "Clark decided that he must turn his titanic strength into channels that would benefit mankind. And so was created, Superman! Champion of the oppressed, the physical marvel who had sworn to devote his existence to helping those in need!" He nearly loses his balance and falls out of my window as he reads the comic to me.

"The butler produces a concealed weapon! 'Reach for the ceiling quick!' he says. 'Put that toy away!' says Superman." C.E. pauses and looks at me again.

"Seriously, Missy," he whines. "There are only two weeks left before school starts. We have to fish before the days are too short to go to the creek."

I look in his direction. I lift my hand, which holds a letter. C.E. squints to see the return address. He presses his glasses back up his nose.

He leans back out the window. "Oh, I see. I better let you go then," he says. But he does not move. He bounces a rubber ball he grabs from off my desk against the windowsill.

C.E. understands the letter is from Daniel L. Button, my dad. On "letter days," as we call them, I cannot seem to get myself out of a depression.

"It's been a while since the last letter day. Are you sure you don't want me to finish telling you about the Superman comic?"

I nod to say, *Yes, I'm sure I don't want you to tell me about the comic.* Instead, he takes my nod as *Yes, please stay in my window and tell me about the comic you memorized by reading it a gazillion million times!* I think he knows what I mean, but he stays anyway. He knows a good hero story is what I need to take my mind off the letter.

Twenty minutes later, he finishes the second comic. C.E. is so worked up reading there is sweat on his brow. "He went to war and punched an airplane! Can you imagine?" he says in wonder.

Knowing I would not answer, he continues to tell me the end of the story, "And so, due to the conciliatory efforts of Superman, the war is halted."

"What a great story." He smiles and shakes his head in disbelief.

I can tell he is wearing his homemade Superman T-shirt again underneath his regular buttoned shirt. He always seems more confident when he wears it (secretly wears it, I mean). I do not think I am supposed to know when he wears it. It is a ratty white T-shirt with the Superman logo in red and yellow with a big "S" in the middle. Thinking about that T-shirt gives me the giggles.

He looks down underneath his buttoned shirt and then back at me and realizes why I am laughing. He probably would start crying if my laughing had not brought me out of my depression. By now it is nearly dinnertime.

I sit up in bed and ask, "Can I treat you to a moon pie at the corner market? Those were great stories. Maybe we'll find another comic while we're there." I take a handful of quarters from my middle dresser drawer. His face beams as I follow him out the window.

I pedal my banana bike while he stands on the axle behind me with his arms outstretched. The sun is still warm on our faces. It makes me sad to think that summer is nearly over. Howard chases us to the corner market, barking the entire time.

As we wait in line to pay for the moon pie, we try to make up our superheroes, discussing what we would call them and what kind of superpowers they would have. Phillip Hill is behind us, and he hears us talking about our hero Firedust.

"What if he," Phillip begins to say, and I clear my throat. He laughs and starts again. "What if she or he has a healing ray?"

"Hmm," we both say as we place our hands on our chins in wonder.

C.E. decides that he wants a banana moon pie instead of the chocolate one he picked, and he leaves the line to exchange it. It is time to pay, and I have nothing to purchase. I let Phillip go ahead of me.

"Thanks, Missy. And I think Firedust should be a woman. She should also have the ability to turn fire into money or produce a healing rain," he says while he pays for his bag of chips.

"Those are great ideas," I say, quite impressed.

"Yeah, last summer C.E. and I were trying to make our comic book, but we couldn't come up with any ideas. Those were the best ideas for superpowers that we had," Phillip says as he takes his bag. He waves to C.E. and then to me.

C.E. reaches the register in time to pay this time. Kimi checks us out, and she keeps entering the wrong code in the register. I look to see what the problem is and find Kimi flirting with C.E. She keeps blowing large bubbles with her gum and sucking them back in.

"Wow, Kimi. You are quite talented with a wad of gum," he says. He pushes the moon pie over to her. "The moon pie? I believe it's thirty cents," he politely says. She snaps her attention back to the register. She gives him back the change from his dollar and brushes his fingertips.

My mouth opens wide. *Ugh!* I grab his hand, and we head for the door. I notice the Bennett brothers walking toward the corner market. They stop to pet a dog tied up to the fire hydrant. Howard is across the street sitting in front of the paint store. I am relieved.

I grab C.E., and we hit the floor behind the Slurpee fountain. After the Bennetts walk into the store and make their way to the paper aisle, we crawl out the door. When we're outside, we look through the window and watch them help a lady with the bag of items that spilled out onto the floor.

When they hear the store door open and hit the bell at the top, they turn. We quickly duck and crawl to my bike. I jump on, and C.E. runs and pushes to get us a fast start. He jumps on, and I ride as fast as I can. Howard catches up to us at the bridge. I am swearing the Bennetts' name under my breath the whole way home; Kimi's too. *Touching C.E.'s fingertips! Ugh!*

We reach his house, and he jumps off the bike and looks at the dust from the driveway. "That was nearly as fast as a speeding bullet!" he says.

I turn my bike around to head for home when I notice he is pacing with his hands on his head. My legs are weak, and my heart is jumping. I start to mention this to C.E., but he interrupts my thought. "I feel stupid running and hiding from those jerks. One of these days, I will stop being afraid and find the courage like ...." He trails off.

I slug his shoulder and say, "I think you're already like Superman. You just haven't tried out all of your super-powers yet."

He beams and slugs me back. "So, what superpowers have I tried out? You said I haven't tried out *all* of them yet." He takes off his glasses to clean the dust off.

"Your ability to make anyone feel good about themselves. Turn a bad day into a good day," I say. He gives me the sweetest smile, his C.E., sweet-as-a-baby, "I love you for-ever" smile. The kind that darn near kills me.

"Thanks," he says.

I pedal past my turnoff to home and decide to go to the town library. I go to the filing cabinet to research irregular heart symptoms when Nickel Silverman bumps into me carrying a load of books on the times and travels of Mag-ellan. They fall to the ground, and I lean over to help him pick them up. He looks over toward the study area. I follow his gaze and see that he is looking at Penny Copperfield.

I clear my throat. "A little light reading over the sum-mer, Nickel? I mean Nick," I say, trying to distract him.

"Huh, what?" he says, pushing his glasses up his nose. He notices me looking at Penny. "Oh yeah, Magellan. Great guy. Full passport, I imagine." He laughs.

I notice Penny peeking over her book at us. Her forehead is as red as her hair. She is either embarrassed or jealous.

"So are you going to the dance?" I casually ask as I help Nickel up with his large load of books. He starts to fall back, and I steady him. He peeks out from behind the stack at me and then again at Penny.

In a very quiet and scared voice, he asks, "Are you asking me?" His voice cracks a bit.

I gasp then look at Penny. "No! I just meant are you going, and if you are, are you taking Penny?"

He shuffles toward the return bin, and I follow him. He whispers something to me, but I do not understand. I ask him again. While he drops the books into the bin, he yells, "I want to take Penny, but I'm afraid to ask her!"

I look down at my feet and clear my throat. His echo reverberates a bit throughout the whole library. We look over to see if Penny happened to hear. She slips a piece of paper over the book she is hiding behind that reads "YES!" with a smiley face next to it.

Nick lets out a sigh, wipes his glasses with his shirttail, and heads off in her direction. I quietly move back to the cabinet to look up heart books. Dandelion comes up to me and asks if she can be of assistance. Dandelion is a volunteer at the library, but I cannot ask her to direct me to the health section. I do not want her to tell Sweet Betty Sue. I do not want her to worry.

I pedal into the sunset and take my time getting home. I leave my bike by the back door instead of parking in the barn tonight.

I drag my feet through the kitchen, take a tub of whipped cream up to my room with a large spoon, and go to bed. Howard hops onto my bed, and I drop a scoop in his dish.

I reread the letter from my dad one more time before I go to sleep. The letter is dated my birthday.

August 27, 1965

Missy Lou:

I won't be able to make it to town for your birthday at this time. I am still in India on business. Maybe next year I will make it for your birthday. I am sending ten dollars to your grandma, and she will place it in your college account at the credit union.

I have something I need to speak with you regarding our family but do not want to write it in a letter. I will call during the holidays, and we will discuss it. I hope the news brings you happiness. I should have told you sooner. I will call on Christmas Day.

Cordially,

Daniel L. Button, CEO

New Generations, Inc.

21st Street

New York, New York

India Office

13b Gashghai Avenue

Bombay, India

Transcribed by
Sanjula Nagina Lahiri

Chapter Seven

What is a hero without love of mankind? —Doris Lessing

I OPEN MY EYES and stare at the ceiling. The clocks chime six. I smell angel food cake. I throw the covers off and fly downstairs to find evidence of a cake. My hair is matted to my head, and I slip on the floor because of my fuzzy socks. I trip and hit the kitchen door because my pajamas are too long. I slide across the kitchen floor and run into the table.

Sitting in the middle of the table is an angel food cake.

"It's a cake!" I blurt out and laugh. "I knew I wasn't crazy." I look at my Sweet Betty Sue. She closes the oven and turns to place another cake on the table. She does not look at me but turns to the freezer.

"Two?" I ask in bewilderment. She opens the freezer to reveal a large mound of cakes, each one wrapped in tinfoil. She takes them out one by one and stacks them on the table.

Her head is still down. "Get dressed. It's time to go to the cemetery," she says without looking at me. I walk backward out of the kitchen slowly. I look at the calendar on the wall and see that it's the first anniversary of my grandpa's death. I feel as if I have just been told he died all over again.

Without a word or any more questions, I leave to get ready for the day. Before I turn, I see my Sweet Betty Sue open the back door. She tenderly loads a mountain of tin-foil-wrapped cakes into a wheelbarrow that is sitting by the back door. It is newly painted baby blue and lined with a tablecloth. I watch her as she takes extra care placing the cakes one on top of the other. Her footsteps in and out of the house sound heavy, and my heart aches for our loss. She looks as though the bandage from a deep wound has been ripped off and a shower of salt is pouring down into it.

Each slow step I take up to my room fills my mind with questions about the cakes. Why are there so many? Why is the attic always locked? Why is she giving me double punishment for the missing cuff? And what is the deal with that cuff anyway?

I dress in my painting overalls to honor my grandpa. I cover my head with my red bandana and head down to help with the wheelbarrow full of cakes.

Sweet Betty Sue's face is forward and brave as we walk the long road down Robison Avenue, across Thimble Creek, and past the town church to the cemetery. She keeps her hands clasped in front of her, and she does not speak a word. The wheelbarrow is starting to give me blisters, and I almost lose three cakes when we cross the bridge. I am relieved that I did not tip over the wheelbar-row. I park it next to my grandpa's war cross and look to my Sweet Betty Sue for direction as she stands behind the tombstone.

She nods toward the cakes, and I begin to place fifty-two angel food cakes on top of my grandpa's grave. Howard starts to howl, which irritates her.

"I want you to get rid of *it* unless you can find the cuff he took and lost!" she snaps.

I am so shocked that she would talk that way to me that I almost don't realize that she is crying. It is rare to see her cry. She is tough as nails and keeps her emotions locked up so tight that if she did not make an angel food cake every Sunday, I would not think that she loved me.

And as soon as I have that thought, I realize that there is a cake for every Sunday my grandpa has not been with us.

I walk up next to her as she carefully arranges the cakes. When I touch her elbow, her body stiffens. She will not look at me. I timidly ask her to tell me why the cuff is so important because maybe it will help me find it. I expect her to say, "Please, just use your imagination, and don't ask me again," but instead she takes my chin in her hands and nods. She smooths her apron and straightens her brooch as she begins telling the story behind the cuff.

"I am not the best seamstress. I can sew on a button in half a minute, knit, crochet, and quilt better than anyone in the county, but I do not sew clothes.

"Your grandpa needed a work shirt when we were first married, and we didn't have the money to purchase one. I spent two days making him a work shirt that he loved so well, he wore it every day. I mended it every weekend, it seemed, and when he went to war, I kept it folded under my pillow.

"When he returned from the war, he continued to wear it every time he painted. The only time he got paint on it was the day your mom died. He dropped his brush for the first time in his career when he got the call that she had passed away. The paint splashed onto his cuff. It would not wash out, but he didn't care. He thought of it as his way to remember your mom. When he decided to stop painting after he was diagnosed with cancer, it hung in the closet until the day we decided to go to town for one last bucket of paint, the day he died."

She looks down her nose at me and says, "I know you've been up into the attic, so I am sure that you found his three books." She kneels at his war cross, clearing it of overgrown grass and weeds.

"He had a book of regrets, which I am proud to say was not more than a page long. But the regrets he did have seemed to haunt him.

"On his last day, we were walking down the sidewalk when he stopped and leaned on his walker. I thought that he was in pain, but he had merely heard something and was listening carefully. He looked to the road and saw that the little deaf girl, Meg, had run into the street to fetch her ball just as the produce truck turned the corner.

"Without hesitation, he threw his walker aside and ran as fast as lightning into that street to snatch Meg into his arms. He made it to the other side of the street before either of them was hit. But when he landed with Meg folded tightly in his arms, he hit his head too hard on the curb.

"I got to his side, and he asked, 'Did I save the little girl?'

"When I told him that she was running to her mom's arms, he smiled and told me, 'I love you one hundred times.' Then he died with a proud smile on his face. His shirt was ruined, except for that cuff. I cut it off and have held on to it this past year."

When I look up at her face, tears are streaming down her cheeks. She too looks proud. I help her up off the ground, and we both turn at a noise behind us.

Meg and her family are walking up the path with flowers. Behind them, Dine and C.E. pull daisy plants in a wagon. I see the Spazzeckis and the members of Sweet Betty Sue's quilting club. Following them are more people from the town being led by the National Guard, a fire truck, the school kids waving flags, and my grandpa's friends dressed in their war uniforms.

Sweet Betty Sue grabs my hand and places her other hand over her mouth. I smile proudly as I watch the procession of people coming to pay respects to my grandpa. They are all familiar faces, each with their special reason for visiting my grandpa on this year's mark. He helped each one of them in some heroic way. I watch as over two hundred connections to my grandpa arrive and stand by our sides.

We are finally able to celebrate his life in the way it should have been done last year if it had not been for the rain.

There is a gun salute, a presentation of the flag to Sweet Betty Sue, and then a song from the children.

> "Soft as the voice of an An-
> gel, Breathing a lesson un-
> heard, Hope with a gentle
> persuasion, Whispers her
> comforting word. Wait till
> the darkness is over. Wait
> till the tempest is done.
> Hope for the sunshine to-
> morrow, after the shower
> is gone. Whispering hope,
> oh how welcome thy voice.
> Making my heart in its
> sorrow rejoice."

I pull on my Sweet Betty Sue's hand. She leans down, and I whisper, "I've heard this song before. Where have I heard it? It came to me in my dream on my birthday."

While the children continue to sing, she whispers in my ear, "After your mother named you Missy Lou Nutmeg Button, she sang it to you before she died. It was her favorite song."

> "If in the dusk of the twi-
> light dim be the region
> afar, Will not the deepen-
> ing darkness brighten the

glimmering star? Then
when the night is upon us,
why should the heart sink
away? When the dark
midnight is over watch for
the breaking of day."

They continue singing as I walk over to my mother's grave. I kneel before her name and touch the engraving with my fingers. I hear the music behind me, and I start to cry.

"Hope, as an anchor so
steadfast rend the dark
veil for the soul, Whith-
er the master has entered
robbing the grave of its
goal. Come then, O come
glad fruition, come to my
sad weary heart, Come, O
thou blest hope of glory,
never, O never depart."

There is a bouquet of daisies, a vase of pink roses, and a small Indian elephant figurine sitting on her grave. A note reads, "To Juliet, Hero, Ophelia, Lady Macbeth and Desdemona—you are always missed." I wonder who has been visiting my mom. I have not been here since my birthday, the day of her death. My school picture still sits

in a little frame against the headstone. I change it every
year on my birthday.

> "Whispering hope, oh how
> welcome thy voice. Mak-
> ing my heart in its sorrow
> rejoice."

The children finish singing. I watch as C.E. and Dine
walk up and place the daisies on the ground surrounding
the headstone. Did Dine place these daisies on my mother's
grave?

I move to the assembly and take my turn to pay my
respects to my grandpa. I tie my red bandana around his
war cross.

Everyone is still and quiet. I look to Dine, who has taken
his hat off. He smiles at me, and I nod to him.

He steps forward and clears his voice. "I can see that
everyone here today has a special connection to Howard,"
he says. "Anyone who has a story to tell, please feel free to
step up and share."

It is still quiet. Dine clears his throat again. "Well, since
I'm up here, I'll go first. Howard is my hero because, during
the war, I lied about my age to get over there and fight.
He did all he could to get me stationed peeling potatoes,
cleaning dishes, or even changing bedpans in the infir-
maries. He watched over me until I turned eighteen. I
went straight to the battlefield. Even then, he kept close
watch over me," he says, wiping his eyes.

Ms. Tovah Stein moves to the front and says with her large voice, "What a great man he was. We ended up on the same bus one day, and there was only one seat left when I got on, the one next to the window that would not close. He gave me his seat and took the empty one meant for me because it had been raining that day. He was drenched by the time we reached town. It was the little things he did that made him such an honorable man."

The mayor takes off his hat and tells us a story about a bad haircut that he got right before a speech and how my grandpa used spray paint to fix the top. Everyone starts laughing. Soon, each person tells their story or act of heroism about my grandfather that has meant something to them. Then it is quiet again.

Sweet Betty Sue wipes her eyes and tells one of her stories. "The first time I ever baked for Howard, I was fifteen, and he had been tutoring me in math. I was so sweet on him. I wanted to impress him with my baking so that he would like me.

"I spent all day making a cherry pie with a beautiful lattice top. I gave him the biggest piece, fresh out of the oven, with a tall glass of milk. He ate the whole piece but drank only half of the glass of milk.

"After he finished tutoring me, he held the side of his mouth and said that he needed to get home to nurse his toothache. He thanked me for the wonderful pie and told me I was making great progress on my equations. He kissed me on the cheek and left my house holding his jaw.

"When I cleaned the dishes, I poured out the remaining milk from the glass and found that it was full of nearly thirty cherry pits. I was so busy making a beautiful pie crust that I forgot to pit the cherries.

"Howard ate the whole thing, pits and all, and even cracked a tooth. I knew from that moment on he was the only man for me. He was a sweet boy and a sweetheart of a man," she says and looks at all the cake in tinfoil. She starts unwrapping them and waving people over to hand out pieces of cake to the crowd.

"To Howard," she says.

"To Howard," everyone repeats.

C.E. and I share the last chunk of cake while we clean up around my grandpa's grave. Everyone has gone home, and the sky is nearly twilight. He gets the wagon, and we walk home with Dine and my Sweet Betty Sue trailing behind us.

"Your grandpa was a hero to a lot of people," says C.E. "He helped me down from a tree one day when I got the back of my shirt caught on a branch. I was dangling for over an hour before your grandpa came to my rescue." He stops the wheelbarrow and helps me in. He pushes me in the wheelbarrow, a bit slower now.

"It's the little things that mean the most," I say. "They add up real fast, don't they?" I look up at his face over mine. He smiles. It makes me want to kiss him, and I get butterflies in my stomach.

We reach the back door, and it takes C.E. longer to help me out of the wheelbarrow than it did to help me in it. By the time I get free, Dine and Sweet Betty Sue are by our sides.

"Dinner is in thirty minutes. You three wash up," she says and holds the door open for us. We make our way to the sink to wash up. While Sweet Betty Sue and Dine are in the pantry deciding what to eat for dinner, I tell C.E. the story of the cuff and why it's so important to find it for her.

C.E. gets a serious look on his face. "That's a heroic story. He was a real superhero." He marvels.

"Yes, he was."

After a fast dinner of ready-bake rolls and soup from a can, Dine heads for home. "Be home by ten o'clock, C.E."

C.E. nods with a mouth full of cake.

"Thanks for dinner, Betty." He pauses. "It was a real nice memorial today. I'm glad I could be a part of it." He puts his hat back on his head and waves.

Sweet Betty Sue waves back to him and then turns her attention to me. "So what are you wearing to the dance tomorrow night?"

"You know I don't have anything to wear. I'm not going," I say and start to cry. I throw my head down on the table. Howard howls while I weep. C.E. shoves the last of his cake in his mouth. He looks like a chipmunk.

"I'll wear my overalls if you wear yours. I don't care," he says, and cake splatters out of his mouth and hits Sweet Betty Sue in the face.

She wipes the cake off her chin and throws her head back to laugh. I struggle for air between my sobs and wipe the snot running out of my nose on my sleeve before smiling at C.E.

"Thanks. I will find a new bandana. Maybe blue? Do you have a bandana to match?" I ask optimistically.

C.E. tries to answer, but Howard continues to howl. He does not notice that I have stopped crying. I shout at him, "Howard, stop howling. If you cannot stop howling, make yourself useful and find that cuff."

I have never been rough with Howard, and I move to hug him after I scold him, but he runs to my Sweet Betty Sue and chews on her apron.

"Howard, stop that now. This is my best apron," she snaps. Not only is it her best apron, but it is her only apron.

He tears the corner of her pocket, and my grandpa's cuff falls out onto the ground. She slowly picks it up and moves quietly from the kitchen. There is a click of the light in the parlor and then another click of the door locking behind her.

I check on her one last time when the clocks in the house chime two in the morning. I can hear the rhythmic clicking of her knitting needles through the door. I think it would be best if I don't interrupt her.

Chapter Eight

Heroism feels and never reasons, and therefore is always right. —Ralph Waldo Emerson

I WAKE UP TO Howard's slobber dripping down my cheek. He is lying over me, still sleeping, when I roll out of bed. I leave him to continue to rest on my pillow. The clocks chime eleven. I have never slept this late except for the time that I had chicken pox. My dreams last night were disturbed with large knitting needles and pink buttons. My heart rattles in my chest. I wonder why Sweet Betty Sue did not wake me earlier.

When I reach the parlor door to check on her, it is already open. I hear her in the button shop writing up an order on a receipt. She passes me in the hall holding a small bag of buttons. At the front door, she turns and looks over her glasses at me. "I finished the quilt. You can give it to Howard. I'm leaving to run this order into town." She leaves before I can say anything back to her.

I look back in the parlor and see the light blue and dark blue squares she has been working on all year, knitted together. The quilt is knitted dark blue with the light blue squares forming an "H." I take it upstairs and place it on Howard. I guess it is my Sweet Betty Sue's way of thanking him for finding the cuff and welcoming him to the family.

After I dress for the day, I go back down to run the shop while Sweet Betty Sue is gone. Most of the customers are finding last-minute buttons for repairs or new outfits in preparation for the dance tonight. By five o'clock, I finish cleaning up and close out the register.

I wait to turn the lights off. I want to peek at my buttons again, but when I can't find them in their usual spot, I realize that they were the special-order Sweet Betty Sue delivered to town earlier. I then notice she has been gone for nearly six hours, and I begin to worry.

I call Dine, and he says that she has just left his house and is on her way home. I think Dine mentions something about the dance that evening, and I feel a sudden lurch in my stomach. My nerves get the better of me, and I hang up on Dine without saying goodbye. I run upstairs and try my best to fix my hair. I open my closet and pull the two cleanest pairs of jeans out and try to decide which one looks the best. I look at myself in the mirror, wearing dirty overalls. I shake my head at my reflection. I give up. It's no use. I fall on my bed and watch the model airplane propellers move in the breeze from the window.

I hear the door open. I can hear C.E. and my Sweet Betty Sue talking in the foyer. C.E. is already at the house to pick me up. My head starts to feel dizzy. I peek over the banister to see Sweet Betty Sue straightening his tie and flattening the front of his suit. I did not even know he owned a suit. I cannot believe he would go back on his word to wear his overalls and show up looking so nice. If I were not so mad, I would swoon over his appearance tonight. He cannot expect me to go to the dance with him now, looking like a farm girl who has been selling buttons all day.

As Sweet Betty Sue starts for the stairs, I run into my room and hide under my red afghan. I kick my shoes off, determined that I will not go to the dance. Slowly, as I sit under my covers, I take off my socks and overalls as well.

Sweet Betty Sue knocks on my door and slowly opens it. She places a long, thin box and a thick smaller box, each wrapped with baby blue ribbons, on my bed.

"C.E. is waiting. Don't take too long getting ready," she says and closes the door behind her.

I open the thin box and pull back the tissue paper. Inside, folded nicely, is a white satin dress. It is the sweetest thing I have ever seen. The sleeves are short and slightly gathered. On the cuffs are buttons, pearl buttons. They match the three pearl buttons going down the front of the dress. They are my buttons, the most beautiful buttons in the world. I dress and look at myself in the mirror. I tie the large blue ribbon around my waist and into a bow in the back. I feel pretty. I even look pretty. I cannot believe I never wear dresses. They are so comfortable. I look down at my grubby high-top shoes and holey socks sitting on the floor. I pull the dress up to show my ankles and walk over to the bed to open the last box.

I take the thick box from the bed and cross my fingers, hoping that it is a pair of shoes. Inside the box is a pair of tan pumps and a pair of nylons. After falling off my bed three times in my attempts to pull on my nylons, I am finally dressed.

After I dress, Sweet Betty Sue comes to get me for the dance. She stands behind me as I look in the mirror. She takes the brush from the dresser and gently styles my hair. She removes the ribbon from the box and ties it around my head.

"You look like your mom," she says, pulling a loose thread from my shoulder. "Your grandpa always thought so too."

I turn around and wrap my arms around her waist and give her the biggest hug I have in me. "Thank you so much, Grandma," I cry. I only call her grandma when I am scared. I start to shake a little bit.

"C.E. is here. He will be by your side tonight. Do not be scared. It is only a dress. You are still the same inside. I know it's hard to grow up, but you're doing a beautiful job of it," she says as she wipes my tears.

I am afraid of growing up. It is all I've ever wanted. Now, I find it much harder than I imagined. Before I can think any more about how frightened I am to go to my first dance, she hands me a boutonniere to pin on C.E.

"I'm nervous," I squeak.

She smiles. "Don't keep C.E. waiting too long," she says before shutting the door behind her. I stand in front of my mirror again. My dress reminds me of the movie, *The Sound of Music*, that C.E. took me to last spring. "Girls in white dresses with blue satin sashes." My grandpa would have loved that show. I miss dancing with my grandpa. As many times as I stepped on his toes, he never said a word about his aching feet. I am a horrible dancer.

I look to the mirror again. *Right, left, right. No. Feet together? Right arm on his shoulder? One, two, three, turn?* Maybe I can convince C.E. to sit and watch everyone else with me instead of dancing.

I take three fast breaths and head toward the stairs. I catch C.E.'s attention away from pulling at his tie, which matches my sash. When I reach C.E., I look up at my Sweet Betty Sue, who leans on the banister above us.

"Thank you for making the dress and tie," I say and twirl.

"I didn't. But I did wrap the bows around the boxes," she says as she winks at us.

I turn to C.E. and pin his flower to his lapel and my finger. I suck on my finger as he fumbles with my corsage. Neither of us says anything as we continue pricking our fingers and dropping the flowers on the ground. Finally, we blurt out nervous laughs.

"Let's try this one at a time," he says. He helps me pin the flower on his lapel, and there are no more pricked fingers. He moves closer to me, and I hold the corsage in place as he pins it to my dress. His fingers are touching my collarbone. My face feels red. I hope it is not. I wonder if he can feel the pounding of my heart. *Please do not faint!*

"There," he says as he steps back to proudly examine his handiwork. Not bad for pinning on a corsage for the first time.

I look down. "Daisies, my favorite. Thanks," I say. He sticks his arm out for me to take, and I link my arm in his. Trying to be so grown up and serious as we leave the house, we both start to laugh.

Outside, Dine is waiting in his horse-drawn buggy that he only takes out for the Fourth of July parade every year. We hop in the back and take a very slow drive to the Town Festival dance.

As we cross the covered bridge over Thimble Creek, C.E. clears his throat. "You look pretty," he says as his voice cracks. He pulls on his tie as if it were choking him. I start to laugh. He leans over and slugs my arm.

When we reach the pavilion, I can see Lizzie Bennett hiding behind her mom, who is next to the stage. The Bennett brothers are facing the stage watching the musicians play when Crystal notices C.E. and me walking toward the dance floor.

"Over here, Missy," Crystal says as she takes a sip from her punch. She nudges Lizzie to turn around and face us. We come face to face with the entire Bennett family. The brothers look at us as though they want to growl or bark. Lizzie cannot seem to make her eyes meet mine.

"You look beautiful," Crystal says. "I love the buttons."

I finally make eye contact with Lizzie, who looks as if she might start crying. I won't blame her either. She is dressed in the pinkest of all pink dresses. Enormously puffy sleeves, lacy collar, lacy trim, lacy hair bow, pink scalloped ribbon, and those darn pearl rose buttons on her cuffs, waist, bodice, and dress trim. Her socks are pulled up to her knees and are also edged with lace. Her white shiny shoes have pink bows at the tops with a button in the center of each. And to match Lizzie are her two nasty, mean, bully brothers wearing pink ties, pink cummerbunds, and pink socks which are visible because their pants are hiked up due to their pink suspenders.

C.E. and I grab each other's hands tightly to keep from laughing. Crystal is radiant in a white chiffon summer gown with a band of pink flowers in her hair. She always seems to wear white. And she always dresses Lizzie in pink. Poor Lizzie. Tonight is the first time since I've known her that I feel sorry for her.

Finally, I gather my strength. "Crystal, your family is radiant tonight. They are so lucky to have such a talented mother as you to make them such beautiful outfits," I say as sweetly as I can while smiling my darling smile.

The Bennett brothers turn red in the face, and Lizzie starts to pout. "Why couldn't you make my dress like Missy's dress?" she cries.

Crystal whispers to Lizzie, "I would have made her dress like yours if I had more time."

"You made my dress, Crystal?" I ask, quite shocked. She begins to fidget with Lizzie's outfit until Lizzie slaps her hands away.

"It was nothing. Betty came by with the fabric today and asked if I could make something simple but sweet. I wish I could have dolled it up a bit more like Lizzie's. I hope you are still happy with the dress, even though it isn't as breathtaking as Lizzie's," she says apologetically.

"I love it. Thank you," I say, still holding C.E.'s hand. He has been very quiet this whole time. I squeeze his hand, and he begins to pull me away.

"Well, we all came to dance. Let's hit the dance floor. Do you know how to waltz, Missy?" he asks as he offers me his arm. He turns and looks at Lizzie as we leave. "You look good in pink, Lizzie," he says, which makes her blush.

She curtsies and replies, "I like your haircut, C.E. I can see your eyes."

I get a weird feeling in my stomach that makes me want to set her hair on fire. I pull hard on C.E.'s arm and drag him to the dance floor. I throw his arm around my waist and place my hand on his shoulder. I do not know how to dance but watch the others around us. I will dance all night if it keeps C.E. away from Lizzie. We start moving to the rhythm of the music, and I glare at him when he turns to look at Lizzie.

"Why did you have to be nice to her?" I say with anger in my voice that shocks both of us.

He shakes his head at me and says, "She looked like she could use a compliment tonight, Missy," he explains. "How would you feel being dressed in Pepto Bismol? I imagine I would be feeling a little stupid tonight and not have any fun at my first dance." I slug him on the shoulder and laugh. I step on his toes a few times and see him wince. He only smiles at me, never saying a word.

Penny and Nick are dancing circles around us. I notice Leonard, Phillip, and Charlie at the dessert table discussing superheroes' abilities. I notice C.E. watching them, wishing he were with them. I have never had a problem sharing C.E. with our other friends, but tonight I just want to be with him alone. It is nearly the end of the dance. C.E. gets some punch for the both of us, and we make our way to the front of the stage.

Lizzie sings her Italian aria flawlessly. She does not seem to be self-conscious about her appearance anymore, and the entire time she sings, she looks at C.E. He smiles back and claps the loudest when she finishes.

I feel I have grown in the last few weeks. But just because I have realized I bullied Lizzie for so many years and promise to stop does not mean I forgive her for all the bad things she's done to me. I do not want to feel like I owe her anything. I will not let her dance with C.E.!

I can forget the time she cut a chunk of my hair off in second grade and used it as a bookmark. I can even forget the time she put worms in my sandwich. Flirting with C.E. is too much. She has gone too far. This is far worse than fifth grade when she placed a whoopee cushion on my chair during a spelling test while I went to sharpen my pencil.

Lizzie sits down on the side of the stage as Ms. Tovah Stein sings her song. Her large voice echoes through the pavilion, the town, and possibly to the next city. As she sings "Sylvia," Lizzie acts as though the song is about her, gaining C.E.'s attention as I listen to Ms. Tovah Stein.

"Sylvia's hair is like the
night, Touched with glanc-

> ing starry beams, Such
> a face as drifts thro'
> dreams, This is Sylvia to
> the sight."

She sings three more verses and one chorus. About the time I think about reaching down to throw my shoe at Lizzie's face, Ms. Tovah Stein stops singing, and the crowd wildly applauds. She blows a kiss to me, and I wave to her.

C.E. moves us toward the stage where Lizzie is exiting. I grab his arm and storm away from the festival to the carriage where Dine is waiting for us. I want to stop feel-ing like I'm going to scream at any moment or clobber C.E. with my other shoe.

The ride home is long because we are in a horse-drawn carriage and because of the ache in my heart. I feel strange and unusual. I never thought of C.E. as anything more than a friend or even a brother. He is my best friend, and now my stupid feelings are going to mess it all up. I cannot control my anger when he turns his attention to Lizzie. I am mad that he feels anything for Lizzie and that I am jealous. I guess Lizzie finally got what she wanted after all these years, to make me jealous of her. Now I know exactly how she has felt about me all these years, even if I have never understood why. I can hear my heart beating in my head, and it is fast. C.E. leans his face on his hands and watches the tall grass hit the carriage as we move down my driveway. He lets out a heavy sigh.

Before the carriage stops, he jumps out to run around and help me down. I slap his hand away and start running for the back door. He runs after me and catches me by pulling one of my braids to stop me before I can grab the door.

"Ow! C.E.!" I yell as he pulls me by my hair and turns me around to meet his face. He grabs me by the shoulders and leans in to kiss me. But he closes his eyes before his lips reach mine, and he misses. He kisses my nose, which he presses up with his lips, making me look like a pig. I am not sure he noticed that he kissed my nostrils.

He locks eyes with me as I try to turn my face away. "Missy, you're the only girl for me," he says. "You always will be." He steps back and watches me wipe the slobber off my nose. "And don't worry, I won't try kissing you again until your birthday." Then he slugs my arm as he runs back to the carriage.

I climb into bed after doing a lousy job of brushing my teeth. Howard lies on top of me, and I drift off to sleep.

My dreams are restless. I dream I cannot find the key to the attic. I kick down the door to find that my mom's hope chest is missing. I cannot stop spinning, and when I finally stop, the attic is empty and freshly painted pink. Then I run to C.E.'s house, only to find that the tree house has burned to the ground, and the daisies he planted are wilting and dripping pink paint. I wake myself up as the clocks chime half-past three. The crickets are still chirping in the dark. I curl myself into a ball while I try to bring my heart rate back down while breathing in through my nose and out my mouth. I start to count all the things I am doing tomorrow with C.E. to calm myself into sleep again.

My last thought is how much I hate the color pink.

Chapter Nine

I believe it is the nature of people to be heroes, given the chance. —James A. Autry

I CANNOT SEEM TO open my eyes. There is faint beeping in the distance. My covers feel strange on my body. Why am I flat on my back? Why isn't Howard next to me? I pull my eyelids apart and see a speckled ceiling. Everything is white. I try to raise my arm to touch my forehead and wince in pain.

I turn my head slowly and notice a cast on my forearm. I use my other arm to touch my forehead, which feels like it is splitting in two. There is a five-inch row of stitches from the middle of my forehead down to my right temple. The more conscious I become, the more pain I am in. I look at my arm that is not in a cast and see an IV. I follow the tube up to a bag hanging on a pole. I start to breathe fast as it dawns on me that I am in the hospital. The slow rhythmic beeping is now racing.

Then I hear a commotion, and a nurse runs to my side. She shines a light in my eyes and asks me a question I do not understand. My hearing is thick and clouded. There is another nurse in the room, and I am pinned down to the bed as I begin to kick and scream. I feel a needle jab my arm, and my head spins. A million stars are chasing me as I fall into darkness.

My eyelids are wet and sticky. I can taste blood. I am afraid to open my eyes again. The beeping noise is still there, and it gradually gets faster. Before I can panic again, Sweet Betty Sue shushes me softly and says, "Missy, it's going to be OK. You have been unconscious for two days. I was afraid you wouldn't wake up." I hear her sniffle.

I start to cry but refuse to open my eyes. *Why am I here? I try to remember what happened the day after the dance. I can visualize small things, and then I see C.E. I shift my weight in the bed, and my legs feel bruised. What was I doing? Remember. You must remember.*

Then my memory comes back to me as if I had been splashed with a pail of cold water on a winter day.

C.E. and I went to town the day after the dance to check out the new comic at the drugstore and to split a milkshake. "Charlie Hoon said the comic is about Johnny Thunder's evil Earth-1 counterpart," he said in an excited rush, "who seizes control of the magical Thunderbolt and journeys back in time to prevent the origins of the Justice League's membership. The Justice League is forced to battle the Lawless League of Earth-A." He was breathing hard as he opened the door to the store.

The comic turned out to be an empowering comic where the superheroes had to fight for their right to be superheroes. After splitting two milkshakes one right after the other, we decided to reread the comic down by the creek while we fished.

On our way out of the store, we walked right into the Bennett brothers. Their faces looked like they had sucked on a lemon rind too long, and they were angry about it. I heard C.E. swallow. My heart started to race. I knew that we were in trouble—but not the kind of trouble where we would have our chewing gum stolen; it was the kind of trouble that would leave a mark on us the rest of our lives. They were ready for a fight.

I think they were angry about wearing pink the night before at the dance and wanted to take it out on someone. C.E. and I just happened to show up at the wrong place and time.

Just as fast as we bumped into them, they were pinning us up against the wall outside. They each held us with a fistful of our shirts and the other fist waving in our faces.

"Leave us alone. We haven't done anything to you," C.E. yelled with loud confidence in his voice. He was thrown against the wall even harder the second time. Then the younger Bennett brother copied the older, and I was pushed back against the wall too. "You leave her alone!" C.E. yelled even louder. He tried to wriggle free but was slammed back harder.

"What are you gonna do about it?" The older Bennett brother laughed. He pulled the comic from C.E.'s back pocket. "You like baby stories?" he asked, and C.E. grabbed the comic back from him, making him mad.

"I'm warning you. I will not take this anymore. Leave us alone," C.E. calmly stated.

The younger Bennett brother pulled on my braids when I tried to escape. C.E. found the strength to overpower the older Bennett brother, who was near twice his size, by kicking him in the shin. "Run!" he cried to me as both Bennett brothers ganged up on him, leaving me unguarded and free to run.

When they both grabbed C.E. from the back, one on each shoulder, I stopped and turned to help him. I did not know what I was going to do, but I had to go back. I heard a scream and froze where I stood.

Crystal and Lizzie came around the corner from the fabric store and witnessed what was happening.

"What are you doing?" she screamed. I thought she was yelling at her sons. "C.E., don't let them treat you that way. Show them what you're made of, kid," she yelled, tossing her bags to the ground, and running toward her sons.

C.E. looked down the road and then back at me. "Run!" he screamed.

I did not want to run away from him. He was frantic. He yelled again, but I gradually made my way back to him to get those Bennett brothers off him.

What I only later realized was that C.E. had seen a Greyhound bus speeding down the street. He did not want me to run away. He wanted me to run out of the street to safety. He struggled against the Bennetts and panicked when he noticed which direction I was headed.

C.E. tried again to break free. He threw back his head, knocking it into one of the Bennett brothers and giving him a bloody nose. Crystal got to her sons and tried to release their grips, but they would not let go. The bus was getting closer.

The older Bennett brother grabbed C.E.'s face, tearing his glasses off. Then, as if straight from the page from a comic, C.E. ripped his shirt off, buttons and all, to get out of their grasp, revealing his homemade Superman T-shirt. "Missy!" he yelled.

My last memory before waking in the hospital bed was seeing C.E. next to me on the street, staring straight up at the sky without blinking, with blood slowly dripping out of the corner of his mouth.

My heart races. I open my eyes and see my Sweet Betty Sue sitting next to me, holding my hand. I look around the room. C.E. is not here. Where is he? *Where is he?*

"Grandma," I scream, "where's C.E. Where is he? Grandma, where's C.E.?" The nurses run in again. Sweet Betty Sue tries to calm me down. I see a nurse with a shot.

"No, please don't. I just need to know where he is," I plead. I look at Sweet Betty Sue and see her worried face. Her hand strokes my brow.

"You need more rest," she cries, and the nurse gives me another shot in my arm.

When I wake up again, Sweet Betty Sue is sitting in my room with Dine, Ms. Tovah Stein, and Crystal. They have all been crying but smile with relief when they see me sit up in bed on my own. I stay as calm as I can to prove I can be awake.

After the doctor checks on me, he encourages me to try and rest. I cannot keep my eyes off Sweet Betty Sue. I look to her for the answers I know she is waiting to tell me. She knows that I am anxious about C.E.

Once the doctor leaves the room, she looks to Dine, who wipes his brow. He blows his nose in his handkerchief and nods to her. She tells me about the accident.

"C.E. saw that bus coming straight toward you. He ran as fast as he could to shield you from the impact and was able to push you to the other side of the street where you fell against the fire hydrant and then onto the pavement. C.E. was hit by the bus and landed next to you. You screamed and screamed and grabbed at his shirt trying to wake him, and then you finally passed out." She starts to cry. Crystal goes to her side and takes her hand. I wonder why Crystal is here but assume that it is because this is her sons' fault.

I look to Dine, tears streaming down my face. "Where is he?" I cry. "Please tell me." I gasp for air and feel my chest tightening again. Dine walks over to me and grabs my hand.

"I'm sorry sweetie, but he's in a coma. The doctors are not sure he will ever come out of it. He hit his head hard. They aren't sure if he has the strength to heal himself."

"I want to see him. Now!" I cry angry tears. I try to pull the IV, the oxygen, and all the other tubes off me as quickly as possible.

Dine gives me a sympathetic smile, and the women try to help me back into bed. I slap their hands away. "It's no use fighting me. Get me a wheelchair and take me to C.E., or I will crawl," I say.

Dine stretches out his soft, sun-weathered hand. "Ladies, I believe she asked for a wheelchair," he says, and they scramble out of the room. He helps me to my feet, and I must grab his waist to keep from falling. "Whoa now. Slowly, Missy Lou," he says calmly.

Crystal argues with the nurses out in the hall but soon comes back into the room with a wheelchair. Sweet Betty Sue and Ms. Tovah Stein help me into the wheelchair, even though I can tell they are worried about me.

"Thanks," I say and look up at Dine after I have all my tubes and IV wrapped properly around myself in the chair. "Please take me to him, Dine." He nods and pushes me out of the room.

The elevator to the third floor, where the Intensive Care Unit is, seems like it is moving at a snail's pace. When the door opens, I motion to Dine and plead, "Go, go, go." He squeezes the chair through as the doors open too slowly.

When we reach the nurses' station, I can tell by the looks on the nurses' faces that I am not supposed to be here. I look at them and point my thumb into my chest, threatening anyone who comes close to me, and say, "I'm the best friend."

Dine wheels me next to his bed, and everyone leaves me alone next to the curtain hanging around his bed. I slowly move the curtain to see C.E.'s face. He is bruised like I am and has a stitched forehead like mine, but he has a slanted line that connects one temple to the other. His face is so swollen that I cannot see the freckles under his eyes.

I smooth his hair and outline his face with my fingers. I rest my head on his arm, which is in a cast like mine, and I fall asleep. When I wake, I look around the room and remember where I am and why. The windows are dark, and the hallways are quiet. I feel lonely, and a chill is slowly creeping over my body. I lean over and kiss C.E. on the cheek.

I try to wheel myself out of the room but turn the wrong way and right into his nightstand. I see a vase full of daisies and smile knowing that they are from Dine. Tucked behind the vase is a small card from Lizzie. My heart does not race. I am not jealous or angry now. I would even be happy if C.E. married Lizzie if only he would wake up. His comic is also on his nightstand, taped together with tender care. It brings back the last memory I had before I blacked out in the street.

When the bus hit C.E., the pages of his new comic book went flying in the air and floated down on us as we lay on the street. I relive this vision in my head again. And again. Thinking back to the accident makes me nauseous.

I want to slug C.E. on the arm to say goodbye like we usually do but instead give him another kiss on the cheek. When I wheel myself out of the room, Sweet Betty Sue is sitting in the hall and knitting. She places the yarn in her bag and rises to meet me, bending down to my level and taking my face in her hands.

"Never lose hope. Never," she says and cleans my face with her handkerchief before wheeling me back to my room.

After I eat my dinner, I realize that I have not seen or heard Howard since the accident. I cannot remember if I took him with us to town that day, and I'm scared that he might have been hurt too.

"Where's Howard?" I ask Sweet Betty Sue after drinking my milk.

"He's downstairs waiting outside the hospital doors. He has not left since the ambulance brought you in. He started howling when he heard the sirens and kept tugging at my apron until I followed him. We got to the accident right as they were loading you and C.E. into the ambulance. I climbed in and rode with you, but since dogs are not allowed in ambulances, he ran the entire way, following until we arrived here. Between Dine and me watching over him, he's had plenty to eat and drink. I even brought his blanket and my large umbrella to keep him shaded," she explains and smiles sweetly at the thought of him.

I fall asleep easily, knowing Howard is waiting outside for me to get well. I still wake up crying and aching for C.E. throughout the night.

After two more days at the hospital, it is time for me to go home, but I am not ready to leave C.E. The ride home is quiet. Howard lays his head in my lap, and I stroke it slowly. The roads are covered with yellow and red leaves that fall from grieving trees. It seems like even the earth is sad.

The wind has such a sharp chill to it that I close the window in my bedroom for the first time in months to keep the bitterness out. I stand and look through my telescope toward C.E.'s treehouse. Closing the window makes me feel I am closing C.E. out though, so I open it again and put on an extra pair of socks to keep me warm.

I go to sleep without dinner. I have no appetite, even though Sweet Betty Sue has made me angel food cake for my meal, hoping that it will get me to eat something. I do not want anything. I want C.E. He is my life. He is everything to me. I am sure I can't live without him.

Chapter Ten

What makes a hero truly great is that they never despair. —Roy Thompson

SINCE THE HOSPITAL IS only five miles from my house, I get up every morning and ride my bike to visit C.E. Today is my fourth day making the trip. I pack my bag with lunch and some dog biscuits, and Howard and I head out before the clocks finish chiming at seven. It is not easy to ride a bike with a broken arm, but I do it anyway. I know C.E. would do the same for me. I stop at his house, grab all the comics that he owns, and pack them in my bag. Dine puts a large pack of gum in my bag and hugs me before I leave.

I set out the umbrella, Howard's blanket, and food for the day before heading up to the ICU on the third floor. I read C.E. four to five comics a day, trying to be as animated as he always was when reading to me. I try to do all the voices as I read. I sound and look silly, but it makes me feel closer to C.E., and I feel like he can hear me somehow.

The ride home from the hospital is always hard for me. I never want to leave C.E., and I feel so lonely when I leave him. I ride directly into the sun and it makes it hard for me to see oncoming traffic. I shake the whole way home because of my nerves. I am not sure I'll ever be the same around traffic again, at least around Greyhounds.

After two more days of making the round trip on my bike with Howard by my side, Sweet Betty Sue drives me on Sunday, when visiting hours are shorter and not worth the long bike ride.

To pass the time before I can visit C.E. again, I sulk around the house. Sweet Betty Sue offers to help me paint the kitchen when she notices I need something to occupy my time. I forget that I have not painted the kitchen for the trouble Howard got me in earlier this summer.

We listen to Doris Day and Rosemary Clooney's records for the first hour that we paint. After what must be my tenth yawn, Sweet Betty Sue turns on the radio to my favorite station. After a while, C.E.'s and my favorite song comes on, and I start to sing. Singing passes the time, but it also makes me anxious to visit C.E.

In the evening, I sit in the parlor with my Sweet Betty Sue and make a necklace out of our "Take a button, leave a button" jar.

"That's quite nice," she says, looking at my handiwork while I inspect it in the light. I put it around my neck to see if it is long enough.

"You have an eye for mixing those buttons with the beads. You could sell those in the store, I bet," she says, returning to her knitting.

I finish by putting a nice clasp on it to make it look more professional.

"Maybe I'll show this to Ms. Tovah Stein. She would know if customers would buy stuff like this," I say.

After I finish the necklace and a matching bracelet and earrings, I head up for bed. Before I close my eyes to sleep, I plan.

> "To the world you may be
> one person, But to one per-
> son you may be the world."

This morning I pack my bag for the day to visit C.E., but I pack my pajamas, an overnight kit, enough packs of Double Bubble gum to last a year, and a few comic books from the drugstore. I am determined not to leave C.E.'s side until he wakes up.

I say goodbye to Sweet Betty Sue. She grabs her keys and purse. "Missy Lou," she says, blocking me from leaving the house. "Let me drive you. You can call me if you need any more provisions from home. Now, run upstairs and bring your red afghan. You'll need something to sleep under because they won't lend you a blanket in ICU." She grabs a large piece of angel food cake, wraps it in tinfoil, and places it in my bag.

When we reach the hospital, she hugs me goodbye. "Tell C.E. I'm thinking about him," she says before I shut the door. Howard comes along again, and we set his bed up outside the hospital entrance.

"Good boy, Howard. I love you," I say and hug him before heading for C.E.

I chew through a pack of gum every hour and read each of the comics to C.E. I take an occasional break to look out the window and check on Howard. I blow the world's largest bubble and am sad that C.E. cannot appreciate it. It reminds me of the bubble that C.E. backed into, resulting in his short hair.

By night, my voice has nothing but a soft scratch. I put on my pajamas and eat the large piece of cake Sweet Betty Sue packed. I curl up at the end of C.E.'s bed wrapped in my red afghan and sleep with my hand on his foot.

When I wake, I read a comic to C.E. before I get dressed. I lie on the end of his bed with the comic above my head and read out loud. I stand on his bed and act out the comic, shaking the mattress when I run in place. "'Those light beams are deadly rays! If one of them were to hit you, you would die,' the Green Arrow says. 'These rays won't bother me, Green Arrow! I'll get you out!' Superman says."

I grab onto C.E. when I act out Superman helping the Green Arrow out of the death rays. I start to act out the climax when the room starts shaking violently, and the bed moves. I throw my body onto C.E.'s and shield his head as the whole building quakes.

"I won't ever let anything hurt you, C.E. I will save you!" I scream. His IV pole falls onto my head, and we crash against the wall. The bed knocks the wall a few more times before there is a calm stillness. Just as fast as the earthquake started, it has stopped.

My heart beats so fast that I can feel it vibrating as I lie on C.E.'s chest. Is my heartbeat irregular, or can I feel C.E.'s mixed with mine? Either way, there is a pounding in my head. I grab C.E.'s head to make sure he isn't hurt, and his eyes are open.

"C.E.," I whisper. "I'm here. Can you see me? Can you hear me? It's Missy." He blinks a few times and licks his lips.

"Missy?" he says with an exhausted voice. I cry for joy and wrap my good arm around his neck and raise him. He slowly wraps his good arm around me.

"I had the weirdest dreams," he says. Then he looks around the room and back at me. "What happened?" I tell him that a bus hit him when he was saving my life.

"No, what happened at the end of the story?" I get a fit of giggles, and he starts to laugh too, causing him to wince in pain.

"Oh, sorry!"

By the end of the day, four different doctors have come in to check on C.E., three nurses have tended to him, and I am still in my pajamas when everyone arrives to see him.

Sweet Betty Sue gives C.E. the quilt she was knitting the other day. It is royal blue with the Superman emblem in the middle in the colors of red and yellow. Crystal gives him boxes of chocolates and two Spider-Man comics, which are probably really from Lizzie. Dine just sits at his son's bedside and smiles and laughs harder than I have ever seen him do before. The hospital even let Howard up to the room for an hour to visit C.E.

After a few more days at the hospital, he is free to go home. Our first adventure after the accident is simply hanging out at the creek, fishing as best we can with our injuries from sunup until sundown. This is how we spend the last few days before school starts. Since neither of us can manage climbing into the tree house or riding a bike, we spend most of our time waiting for a fish to take our bait. Other times at the creek, we sing along to the little battery radio C.E.'s dad bought for him. We cross the bridge to head for home and pause to clink arm casts.

"I'll meet you at the bridge tomorrow for school. Don't be late," I say. I swing my pole around and start to leave.

"Missy," he says, stopping me. "I knew you were there. Or at least I knew that I was safe because I heard your voice the whole time I was in the coma. Thanks for being there for me. I think you pulled me out from wherever I was."

His voice melts my heart. "Thank you for pushing me out of the way of that bus."

"Any time," he says and pauses, deep in thought. "When you told me the story about your grandpa saving Meg, I didn't understand how anyone could risk their life for someone else. But when I was on the sidewalk, watching that bus head straight toward you, the only thing I could think of was how much time I had to get to you. I knew I could do it because your grandpa showed me it was possible."

"Thanks for telling me that," I say. We clink casts one more time and head our separate ways. I feel a little spring in my step for the first time in weeks. I even forget how worried I am about starting school tomorrow. I figure that if I have C.E., there isn't anything I can't do. I turn to watch him walk toward his house. He turns at the same time, and we both wave one last goodbye.

Chapter Eleven

We must become the change we wish to see in the world. —Mohandas K. Gandhi

THE SCHOOL BELL RINGS, and we slam our lockers and head off to English. C.E. is telling me about the new Spider-Man comic he received from Lizzie when we run into her brothers because we are not watching where we are walking. C.E. and I had both forgotten about these two, the reason we were both badly injured and C.E. had been in a coma. The Bennett brothers caused us so much grief the last few weeks that I cannot believe we had not thought about them until now.

Our casts knock them in their stomachs as we collided. "Ouch! Watch where you're going!" the older Bennett brother says. When he realizes that it is us, he leans toward C.E. with his fist clenched. "Next time, I will be the bus, and I won't brake." He punches his fist into his palm.

I cannot believe that they do not say sorry or show any remorse for nearly getting us both killed. I know that Crystal has probably demanded that they apologize, and they probably swore to her that they did, but it still amazes me that they are unaffected by their actions.

C.E. holds the door to the classroom open, and I start to walk in when we hear a thud against one of the lockers down the hall. We turn to see the Bennetts picking on Charlie and Leonard. I pull on C.E.'s good arm. I do not want to get into a fight with the Bennetts on the first day of school. C.E. hands me his backpack and calmly walks over to them. I hang back, afraid but still wanting to know what happens.

The older Bennett has Charlie up against the lockers, and Leonard is on the ground picking up his books. "Your moms will always be maids. You people will never amount to anything but servants," the older brother taunts.

The younger brother laughs. "Yeah, if there were cotton fields out here, maybe you two could get a job. No one else will hire you," he says, and they high-five.

C.E. helps Leonard up off the ground and tells him, "I heard your mother play the piano at the festival. She is talented. Didn't she study in New York, where she obtained a doctorate in music? I heard she was the top composer in her class"

Leonard stands up tall and brushes his shoulder. "Yes, she is an accomplished musician. She gives lessons at a music studio in Orville and plays the piano with the Philharmonic," he says. The older brother lets go of Charlie and walks over to C.E. to look down on him. C.E. turns toward Charlie, who unknots his shirt.

"I thought it was great of your mom to volunteer with the cleanup of Centennial Park," C.E. says casually. "I know she is busy getting ready for school. What is it she teaches at the university?"

The Bennetts glower at C.E. when the bell rings for class to start. I link Charlie's arm in mine and walk him to class.

"My mother is a civil engineer!" Charlie says proudly, loud enough for the Bennetts to hear.

"Thanks," Charlie and Leonard say as we make our way into class and find four seats together. "We would have stood up to them ourselves, but Principal Hill usually sides with racists," he says as if he has a nasty taste on his tongue. We see Principal Hill walk around the corner, whistling as if he had not seen any confrontation with the Bennetts.

"I know the Bennetts are bullies, but I never would have thought them prejudiced as well," I say. They look at me as if I am defending them. "What? I just do not see where they would have gotten the notion to act that way toward anyone. Crystal is a close friend of both of your moms."

Leonard shrugs his shoulders. "Well, thanks again. You know we would do the same for you anytime. But one of these days, Principal Hill is going to get himself into some serious trouble if he keeps supporting as despicable an institution as segregation. I can't believe Phillip is his son." We all nod in agreement.

Charlie motions for us to lean in closer to him. "I heard a few years back that he and some of his friends got in trouble with the law. I think it had something to do with the attack against a young man outside the synagogue in

1944. He didn't get charged with anything, though, because one of the police officers was in on it," he confides. Before any of us can ask what happened to the person they attacked, our teacher clears her throat, and we all jump.

Before I can whisper to C.E. about the information we heard about the principal, he is passed a pink note, which was handed to him from Lizzie's direction. It reads, "I'm glad you are OK. I was so worried. Welcome back to school." I know it is from Lizzie, but I do not care if she has sent him a note in class. C.E. is alive. What more can I ask for? However, when C.E. smiles and neatly tucks it into his notebook, I cannot help but feel a little jealous. It is not the kind of jealousy that Lizzie still holds for me. I feel sorry for her and wonder if she has any friends. This thought makes me think that maybe I have grown a little, but I still stick my tongue out at her when she turns around to smile at C.E.

By lunch today, Lizzie is so excited to see C.E. that she runs over to our bench underneath the tree. "Only six weeks until the Halloween dance, C.E. I already have my costume picked out. You are going to love it. And so are the judges. I bet I will win first prize again this year." She says the last part in my direction, looking down her nose at me.

"That is great, Lizzie. I look forward to seeing you there at the dance," he responds politely.

She steps back a little, and her face falls. "So, you already have a date?" she asks, looking again at me.

"I'm too young to date. I just figured I would show up and have a good time," he says. Lizzie perks up a little, hoping that he means that he is not taking me to the dance either.

She nervously scratches at her arm as we both sit and stare at her. "Well, I guess I'll see you around," she says.

We both wave to her, but C.E. watches her a little longer before she heads back into the cafeteria.

I pull on his sleeve and clear my throat. "So we have six weeks to make a costume. Should we challenge her?" I ask.

"Go ahead. Let us see who can come up with the best costume," he challenges me. I will show him that my costumes are better than Lizzie's. Secretly, I already started to work on them a week ago. They are going to be fabulous, and I cannot wait to surprise him. However, my smile fades as it dawns on me that I am suddenly competing for C.E.'s affections.

He slugs me on the arm and runs to gym class with Charlie and Leonard. Charlie shows C.E. and Leonard an old Superman comic. C.E. throws his head back and lets out his fantastic laugh, the kind that only I like to get out of him. *Humph.* I grab my bag and catch up with Penny on the way to Literature.

Penny elbows me and says, "S–so, I've got my idea for the Halloween p–party too. I hope you will be im–impressed. What is your co–costume idea?"

I blush because I am still not sure if my idea is clever enough, and I also don't want her to copy me. "Well, something along the lines of goblins or ghosts. You know, the usual." I force a laugh and shrug nervously.

We find our seats, and I pull out a blank piece of paper and start working on the costume design. I will beat Lizzie Bennett this year; I must.

Chapter Twelve

I love the man that can smile in trouble, then can gather strength from distress and grow brave by reflection.
—Thomas Payne

THE HALLOWEEN PARTY IS finally here. I am so excited to show C.E. our costumes that I get to his house an hour before the party. I hide the costumes behind the tree and knock on his door.

"Close your eyes. I have our costumes ready," I say and place my hands over his eyes, walking behind him.

"I thought we were going to see who had the best costume, Missy Lou," he scolds. "I had plans for our costumes this year too. The challenge wasn't between you and Lizzie, it was between us."

I did not realize that was what he meant that day at school. He was keeping the peace between Lizzie and me. I do not want him to know how unsettled I am knowing that he is protecting Lizzie. I remove my hands from his eyes after a few moments of silence.

C.E. takes my hand and says, "Let's show each other the costumes we made, and we'll go in the costumes made by whoever has the best idea." I feel it is fair, especially since my costumes are going to be the coolest and most likely beat his.

I pull out my costumes from behind the tree. "Ta-da!" I say as I unveil two large cardboard boxes cut out and colored to look like buttons. "How cool are these?" I say with so much excitement in my voice that I sound like a mouse squeaking as it runs away from a cat. Howard wags his tail fast. C.E. simply stares at me. I do not understand why he isn't enthusiastic about my buttons. The smile drops from my face as he shifts his weight from side to side.

"I was thinking of something a little more adventurous, Missy." He runs into his house to fetch a large black bag. He opens it and throws a very colorful outfit toward me, a Wonder Woman costume. He starts putting on his Superman costume over his clothes. His face lights up, and he says, "Superheroes! I got the idea from Charlie. He and Leonard are going as Aquaman and Batman. I spent the last six weeks on these. Crystal helped us sew them together." He pulls out wristbands for my costume.

I look at him wearily as I hold up the costume. It is high cut with a plunging neckline. "You expect me to wear this? My bathing suit covers more of me," I say.

"You put it over your clothes, Missy. Crystal also made a cape so that you won't be so cold." He pulls out a thin rope from the bag.

He watches me place the wristbands on and adjust my costume over my jeans. "Those wrist bands are made from Amazonium, the hardest metal known to this galaxy. They can ward off any deadly atomic beams and human bullets." He hands me the rope. "And this is your lasso. Whoever it is wrapped around must tell the truth. It has super strength too, even though it's thin."

I tie the rope to my side with the loop Crystal sewed onto the costume for me. "We didn't even discuss whose costumes we were going to wear. We should at least try on the buttons," I say in defense of my hard work, but Howard starts to growl.

C.E. ties a cape to Howard and then laughs and shakes his head at me. Howard loves his cape. He starts leaping around C.E.'s legs. C.E. walks to my bike and sits down.

"Do you know how hard it was for me to ride over here with those large buttons on my back?" I say, walking to the bike with my hands on my hips. He is still laughing.

"I'll pedal. Hurry up, or we'll miss the games," he says. I give us a head start push behind the bike and hop on the back, holding onto C.E.'s shoulders as my cape flaps in the wind. Howard follows us as we head down the road, passing trick-or-treaters on our way to the school party.

As the sun sets behind us and the school sits ahead in the distance, we feel like real superheroes. C.E.'s chest is puffed up; he left his glasses at home and slicked back his hair. It makes me a little nervous that he is the one steering the bike, but he seems to have more confidence in him tonight than I have ever seen. I feel stronger too, especially since we had our casts taken off last week.

We lock the bike to the rack with the others and walk to the school. We are members of the Justice League of America, and nothing can stop us. Nothing except the

Bennett brothers, and we both hope they will not be at the party.

As the two of us strut down the hallway with Howard toward the gym, our capes billow behind us. and our chests puff up. Through the double doors, walking toward us, are the Bennett brothers.

Not only is it a shock to see them so early in the evening, but they are dressed as superheroes too. The older brother is dressed as the Green Lantern, and the younger brother is the Flash. I assume that when C.E. had Crystal help him with our costumes, she got the idea to dress her boys up as superheroes too. Behind them emerges Lizzie.

I thought she would be dressed as Glinda the good witch from the Wizard of Oz or something oozing with pink, but she is dressed as Black Canary. It all makes sense to me now. Lizzie, along with everyone else in town, knows that C.E. loves superheroes. No wonder she dressed as one herself. I am sure Crystal thought it would be adorable to have the whole Justice League at the Halloween party.

As C.E. and I face the Bennetts, I cannot help but hear my Sweet Betty Sue's old lady music. I hear "Que Será, Será" by Doris Day in my head. I roll my eyes at this useless thought and instead think of "Get Off of My Cloud" by the Who. That's more like it. I use the energy emulating from C.E. and Howard and the strong music in my head to face what I know will be the last stand for C.E. and myself.

We meet in the middle of the hall. Lizzie is smiling at C.E., seemingly oblivious to what we are facing, but neither of us takes too much notice of her now as we see the glare in her brothers' eyes.

"Let us through," C.E. demands.

"No," they say together, pushing him back.

"Stop it," Lizzie says, and she grabs her brothers' arms, having realized what's about to happen.

"We're going to the party. Please step aside," C.E. demands again.

"We have unfinished business with you pukes," they retort.

Lizzie looks frightened. "Please. Leave them alone, or I'm telling Mom." She cries.

C.E. Puffs out his chest and lifts his chin. "For the last time, leave us alone and let us pass."

"Make us," they shout and push both of us back. Howard starts growling. I stand in front of him so that they will not hurt him again.

C.E. gives me the hand gesture for "run," grabs my hand, and gives me a confident smile as we run straight into them, knocking them over. We do not stop. We run as fast as we can to the gym doors. We nearly make it, but our capes are yanked backward. We both start kicking as we are pulled outside. Lizzie runs behind us, crying, and they drag us out to the park near the old well.

They throw us to the ground, and we knock heads. As we rub our skulls, the Bennett brothers lean up against the well and start laughing at us while they load a BB gun.

C.E. elbows me to get my attention. He gives me a cute little smirk. "It all ends tonight," he whispers in my ear.

I shake while holding Howard down to keep him from attacking them. I try to be calm like C.E. but find it hard when I see them load the gun.

Lizzie runs in front of us with her arms outstretched to her brothers. She is crying so hard that no one can understand what she is trying to say.

The older Bennett brother points the gun at us. "Who wants to get shot first?" They are still laughing at us and now at Lizzie too as she tries to defend us. The younger brother pulls her aside.

C.E. stands us up and puts himself in front of me. "Put that toy away," he says, quoting a Superman comic that we read earlier in the summer. Then I hear a bang.

The Bennett brother accidentally shot the gun and looks frantic as he throws it to the ground. He turns to his brother and Lizzie as C.E. falls. "I was only going to scare them. I just pretended to load it," he says, trying to defend himself.

Lizzie and I scream, and I dive to C.E.'s side. He slightly turns his head and winks at me. He pulls me to the ground to help him give the momentum he needs to head straight at the Bennett brothers.

He punches the oldest one in the jaw, causing him to lose his balance and crash into his younger brother, pushing him down into the well. There is a long scream followed by a loud splash. The remaining Bennetts run to the well and look over the side. They try to figure out how to get him out.

C.E. helps me up, and we walk away. He shows me the pie tin that he put under his costume to make him look more muscular. It has a BB lodged in the middle of it.

"You did it, Superman," I say proudly and link his arm with mine. We strut again on our way back to the dance.

We are so excited to get to the party that we start dancing to the music as soon as we can hear it coming from the gym. We are liberated. We have finally defeated our enemies. We both agree that we do not think they will be bothering us anymore. Especially since Lizzie witnessed the whole scene and will tell their mom.

We hear another splash and a scream. Lizzie is in hysterics, jumping up and down in front of the well. The older one went in to help the younger one out, and now they are both stuck. The well is not big enough for them both. They do not have any space to help one another out.

"Please help," she cries.

Without hesitation, C.E. turns around and heads toward the well. He reaches down to the Bennetts.

"Grab my hand." His voice echoes in the well. Their fingertips barely graze. C.E. leans down more, and Lizzie catches him before he falls headfirst into the well too.

"Please help us. He can't swim, and I can't keep treading water for both of us," the older Bennett brother pleads.

Howard barks at me and pulls my lasso with his mouth. I run to the well and throw it down to them. "Hold on to the rope," I yell between all the splashing and crying. "Help me pull," I say to C.E. and Lizzie. The three of us pull as hard as we can. The rope slips once from our grip, but soon both Bennett brothers make it out of the well.

While they are wet and gasping for air on the grass, I tie my lasso around them tightly. They do not try to fight. They are shivering and still in shock.

"This is a truth lasso. You must answer my questions and not lie," I say as I pull the rope tight. They wince.

"Will you ever try to hurt us again?" I ask. They shake their heads. "We saved your lives after you nearly killed us twice! Should you be punished?" I ask. They nod. I look at Lizzie and C.E. and say, "Justice League, what should their punishment be?"

They huddle together and talk for a minute. After they agree, they stand on either side of me. C.E. clears his throat and says, "From this moment, we join forces for good and protect those around us. You will no longer be bullies. And you will apologize to anyone you have ever bullied, starting with Charlie and Leonard."

The Bennett brothers nod anxiously as water runs down their faces. "If you don't agree, Lizzie tells your mom everything." C.E. folds his arms across his chest and stands tall. Lizzie stands with her hands on her hips and sticks her tongue out at her brothers.

As I untie them, I cannot help but feel a little sorry for them. I have realized why I have been a bully, and it never occurred to me until now that the Bennett brothers may have their reasons for picking on kids.

I help them to their feet. The ground beneath them is slushy. They stand shivering, facing C.E. and myself.

The older Bennett brother sticks out his hand and looks down at his feet. He looks up at C.E. and says, "I'm sorry." C.E. grabs his hand and shakes it.

The younger Bennett brother stretches his hand to me, and I take it. "I'm sorry too," he cries and wipes his face with his wet Flash costume. "Friends?"

We all nod our approval. "If we're going to be friends, we need to call you by your first names to make it easier," C.E. suggests. Lizzie gasps and her brothers look at one another.

"You can't do that," Lizzie pleads to C.E.

"Why not?" he asks. "We can't keep calling them the older Bennett brother and the younger Bennett brother. That would be ridiculous."

The brothers lean over to C.E. and whisper. C.E.'s mouth falls open. "You're right. We cannot call you by those names. Then *you* will get beaten up." The brothers look relieved. C.E. snaps his fingers. "I've got it." He points to the older brother. "Your nickname will be Zeke." Then he points to the younger one. "And your nickname will be Heck."

Lizzie places her hand out palm down in the circle we have unknowingly formed. I place mine on top of hers, and one after the other, the boys place theirs down too.

"I've been sick of being called the 'older Bennett brother' for so long. I never thought there was a cool enough nickname to make from Ezekiel," Zeke says.

"Me too. I mean, I was sick of being called the 'younger Bennett brother,' that is. I like how you made 'Heck' out of Hezekiah," Heck says proudly as if he is showing off a shiny toy.

We all turn and walk back to the school for the party. C.E. talks with Zeke and Heck as Lizzie and I trail behind. "I've had lots of practice creating nicknames. It comes pretty easy to me these days," I hear C.E. say.

"So are we going to have a special meeting place for the Justice League?" Zeke asks. "I mean, that is what we are, right?"

"Yeah, and can we dress up more than once a year? These costumes are cool," Heck says as he wrings the water out of his costume.

I slowly wind up my lasso and place it back on my belt loop. Lizzie walks beside me. I feel I should say something but am not sure what. I guess we're friends now. Or at the very least we will be casual acquaintances through the creation of the Justice League.

When we reach the dance floor, C.E.'s and my favorite song is playing. Zeke and Heck head for the cookie trays. I wave to Lizzie and say, "See you later, Black Canary." I smile.

She waves back and replies, "Have fun on the dance floor, Wonder Woman." Then she heads for the back wall with the cup of punch that Zeke has ready for her when she passes him at the refreshment table.

Charlie and Leonard meet us on the dance floor. "Hey, we watched the whole thing!" Charlie says as he slaps C.E. on the back.

"Yeah, way to go!" Leonard says. They both walk toward a group of kids at the punch bowl, and we watch them act out the scene by the well.

I grab C.E., and we dance as hard and fast as we can, looking completely ridiculous. I notice Lizzie looking lonely, so I run to her and grab her by the hand. She drops her cup and grabs my cape, following me back onto the dance floor. C.E. and I teach her our stupid little dance, and the three of us dance around the gym without care. Zeke and Heck finish off the second tray of cookies and watch us from the side. I never realized how pretty Lizzie's smile is when she is laughing. I guess I have never seen her laugh until tonight. C.E. shows off all his crazy dance moves, which keeps Lizzie laughing the whole time.

At ten, Principal Hill announces the winners of the costume contest, "Penny Copperfield and Nickel Silverman for their hard work and creativity." Penny is dressed as a button, and Nick is dressed as a thimble. Everyone claps.

I slug C.E. on the arm. "What?" he says innocently. "We would have won if we had entered the competition," he says, defending himself before I slug him again.

"Thank you for coming. Everyone be safe on your way home," Principal Hill says as the light comes on in the gym.

I shake Penny's hand and congratulate her on the costume award, but she does not seem interested in talking about it. She looks toward Zeke and Heck talking with C.E. as if they are best friends. "I heard what happened. Charlie told me everything." She watches C.E. reveal his pie tin. "Life ca-ca-ca-cannn diminish, or life can empower within a blink of an eye. It's having c-c-courage to make the right decision at the right time that makes the difference," she stutters. Nickel calls for her from the door. She says, "I think having you around gave him the c-c-courage to do what had to be done tonight." She waves to me and skips over to Nickel, who loses his balance when Penny hops on his back and demands a ride out the door.

"Ready to go?" C.E. asks as he walks up next to me with his hands on his hips. "Should we fly or take your invisible airplane?" I start laughing as I bend down and try to wake Howard, who is sleeping under the punch table.

I carry Howard in my arms and wrap his cape around him. When we walk outside, the cold air wakes him up. I sit on the handlebars with Howard in my arms as C.E. starts to head out for the road.

"See you on Monday," Zeke says as he helps Heck with his lock and chain.

"Yeah, at the tree fort after school—I mean the Watch Tower," C.E. replies. He gives a little wave to Lizzie as she follows her brothers on her bike.

C.E. pedals Howard and me home and parks my bike in the barn for me. "Thanks for the ride," I say as I slug his arm. "And C.E., happy birthday tomorrow." I look at my watch. "Actually, *happy birthday* as of three minutes ago. Sweet Betty Sue and I will be over for dinner."

He slugs me back. "Thanks. Make sure you bring the cake," he says as he pretends to fly away.

"C.E.," I call after him. "What do you want for your birthday?"

He turns and a look of relief spreads over his face. "My wish already came true. See you tomorrow. And Missy? Your button costumes were cool. I think they would have beat Penny Copperfield tonight, for sure."

I walk inside with a grin on my face and turn to watch Superman fly away.

Chapter Thirteen

I have friends in overalls whose friendship I would not swap for the favor of the kings of the world. —Thomas A. Edison

THE JUSTICE LEAGUE MEETS every Monday after school at C.E.'s tree house, which we named the Watch Tower. Our meetings mainly consist of playing cards, drinking soda, and reading the latest comic books. The Monday before New Year's Eve, we meet for the first time since Christmas break started. This meeting will be our Christmas party. The League decided that we would not do individual gifts but instead bring five of one thing to the Watch Tower.

While Zeke reads one of his older comics aloud, I look at my five items sitting in front of me on the rug. "After turning the Shaggy Man upon the unstoppable Moon-Being, the League buried them both with another Shaggy Man," Zeke says in a commentator's voice.

I grab my chest as it makes a triple jump. Lizzie leans over and notices that I have lined my gifts in a row. One pack of gum from C.E., a bottle rocket from Heck, an empty can of Coca Cola from Zeke, and a Big Hunk candy from Lizzie. The gift I brought for us I already have pinned to my shirt.

Last week when my Sweet Betty Sue heard I needed to get gifts for today's meeting, she called me into her parlor late one evening.

"These are for the League," she said as she handed me a small bag of buttons. I emptied the bag into my palm. There were five buttons the size of silver dollars soldered onto a lapel pin. Each one had a different superhero on them. I grinned so wide that I think my cavities were showing. I looked at my Sweet Betty Sue, and she was knitting with a smile on her face.

"Sit down. I will tell you a story about the 'Circle of Trust' from when I was young." She continued to knit.

I sat down on the ottoman across from her chair. While I looked at each button, she told me a story from her childhood. At that moment, I was more excited about the story. Sweet Betty Sue had never talked about her childhood or her past. Anything she had to tell me was going to be wonderful.

"I grew up in a workhouse, in a mill. As an orphan, I was not thought of very highly, and no one invested in my education. The same went for any orphan back then. We were all put to work for very low wages. There was a floor supervisor who was very mean to us children and would sometimes lock us up for the day. When any of us needed help or were in danger, we would send each other our buttons. They were all matching but different in a slight way. so that we knew whose button was whose," she said.

"Is that the button you wear on your collar as a brooch?" I interrupted.

"No, that is another story." She looked down her nose then went back to her knitting. "We had a circle of trust. We could trust one another with our lives. When one of us was in trouble and sent out our button, we knew we would be taken care of." She put her knitting down on her lap.

"You have a good circle of friends. I thought those buttons could be your signs within your Justice League," she said, and I hugged her tight.

"Thank you for telling me that story. I love the buttons, I mean pins. And I love the idea of a circle of trust. But I think we should call our circle something different. How about Circle of Strength?" I asked. She nodded her approval. I hugged her around her neck and left the parlor.

I turned to ask her about how she made them since they looked like ferrotypes, but I stopped at the door when I saw her slowly remove her glasses, tighten her eyes, and cover her mouth. Her shoulders started to shake as she sobbed. I wanted to run to her but knew she would bottle her sadness back up and refuse my sympathy. I walked away wondering more about her past than I ever had before.

Lizzie's pin is the Black Canary, Zeke's is the Green Lantern, and Heck's is the Flash. When I took the last two out of the bag, I found that Sweet Betty Sue had engraved the back of my Wonder Woman button with the phrase, "To MY Wonder Woman." C.E.'s pin is Superman. I told them Sweet Betty Sue's story, and we all agreed that if any of us needed help, borrowed strength, or a huge favor, we would do the handshake that we made up the first meeting of the Justice League and leave our button in the other's palm.

Lizzie smooths the front of her pin. "Thank your grandma for the pin. This was nice of her," she quietly says. "I've never had anyone I could trust or rely on. So would you do anything to help me if I handed you this button?" She finally lifts her head to look at me. She looks as though she might cry, likely worrying that I am going to tell her I would not.

In the last few months, Lizzie and I have let our guards down and have grown fond of each other. Some of the things that I've learned about her are that she is more sensitive than I thought, is always fair in her actions, isn't afraid to try something new, is a brilliant mathematician, and is protective of anyone she cares for.

I take the button from her hand and pin it on her collar. "I would do anything for you, Lizzie. And I know you would do the same for me," I tell her.

She throws her arms around my neck and cries, "I would do anything for you!"

The Watch Tower is quiet. Lizzie and I turn our heads and look at the boys. They all roll their eyes at us, and Zeke continues reading the comic while C.E. and Heck play cards.

Lizzie and I start to laugh. "Well, they haven't kicked us out yet," I whisper.

An unexpected snowstorm cuts the Justice League meeting short. Crystal drives off with her kids, and C.E. and I wait out the storm in the Watch Tower.

By six p.m., Dine brings us hot cocoa, cinnamon scones, and bottled peaches for dinner. "Mrs. Henderson's kind thanks for my snowplow job in front of her store and parking lot. Enjoy," he says before he climbs back down the tree.

C.E. and I sit up against the beanbag, wrapped in a plaid wool blanket. We watch the snow silently fall past the window.

Without turning my head, I ask, "Do you remember the time we played hide-and-seek in the snow? You thought you would be clever and hide inside the large snowman we built." I let out a small, reflective laugh. "You were in there for nearly thirty minutes. You were so excited about the great hiding place that you wouldn't come out when I said you were free."

"Yeah, I was too numb to move or say anything. If I had not sneezed just as you were walking right in front of me, I would have frozen to death. I ended up with frostbite so bad on my toes that I nearly lost them. But you sat up against the ottoman in front of the fire all night with me." He looks down at me and smiles.

With a warm and full belly, I lean my head down on C.E.'s shoulder and fall asleep as he reads out of the Emily Dickinson poetry book I brought with me. He reads the passage that is highlighted with the initials GLS next to it. The last entry I hear C.E. whisper is "Hope is the thing with feathers that perches in the soul, and sings the tune without the words, and never stops at all."

It is New Year's Eve, and the clocks chime midnight. C.E. and I run outside and bang on our pots and pans. We spent most of the evening playing Scrabble and making homemade popcorn by the fireplace. The Bennetts were not able to make it to the party because they had all contracted the flu and were in bed resting.

I walk C.E. to the door. On the front hall console is a letter addressed to me. "Have a good night," I tell him. "Sleep tight."

He laughs at me but when I turn around, and he sees the letter, he is as quiet as I am. "Oh, I see," he whispers. He puts on his coat and hat. "It was a great party. I will see you tomorrow.

We can build snowmen. I'll bring the carrots," he says loud enough so that Sweet Betty Sue can hear from her upstairs bedroom.

I am so completely distracted by the letter that I accidentally close the door on my foot. I head up to my bedroom, shut the door, and walk to my window to close the curtains. I see C.E.'s face with steam condensing on the glass. He mouths, "Open up."

He climbs in. I quickly shut off my light, and he switches on the flashlight he uses to walk home in the dark. "I saw the letter and thought you might need me here. I mean—well, I was just anxious for you, I suppose."

We sit on the floor across from one another. I am turning it over and over in my hand. "For heaven's sake

Missy, open it," he finally says. I know he must leave and is worried about getting in trouble.

"No, you open it. And read it please," I plead with him. He rips it from my hand and rolls his eyes at me.

December 25, 1965

Dear Missy Lou,

Merry Christmas. I have enclosed $10 for you to put in your college account. Write to me and tell me about your holidays. I will write later about the family matter I mentioned in my last letter.

Cordially,

Daniel L. Button

C.E. folds the letter and places it back in the envelope. He sits and waits for me to say something. After five minutes of silence, I stand up and open the window for him. "Thanks, C.E. I will see you in the morning. Come early, and I will make your favorite cranberry, oatmeal, pecan, brown sugar, and maple syrup pancakes," I say. He slugs me on the arm, and I slug him back.

"Get some sleep," he says as he climbs out the window. I watch him climb down. "And Missy, it was a great party," he says before he jumps to the ground, grabs his bag, and runs home. I watch his flashlight wobble back and forth through the trees and get my telescope out. When I see that he is at his house, I close my curtains.

I throw the letter in my top drawer and crawl into bed.

∗∗∗

This afternoon, after pancakes and snowmen, I am put to work in the store. I am restocking the Levi buttons and replacement zippers when Crystal walks through the door. She apologizes over and over for coming in on a holiday. Sweet Betty Sue says she is glad for the business and the company. I notice Lizzie sulking in the doorway and run to her side. She offers her hand. We do our handshake, and she leaves her button in my hand.

I look over at Crystal and see that she is buying more pink buttons. Lizzie's face is panic-stricken. I suspect that her mother is planning on making her a new outfit. After getting to know Lizzie over the past few months, I have learned that she hates the color pink. I take the button in my hand and nod to Lizzie.

"Crystal," I say as I approach the counter. "Have you ever thought of creating a dress around a single button?" I can tell I have her attention. She lays the pink buttons down on the counter and turns to me with her hand on her chin.

I walk some buttons over to her and place them in her hand. "This packet of buttons has been here for years. I don't think anyone can create anything to put them on, yet they are one of the most adored patterns." I hand her the packet of red, blue and gold swirled metal buttons. She looks at them and thinks a little longer. "If anyone could figure out a way to use these buttons, it would be you, Crystal."

I leave her with the buttons and walk back to Lizzie. She looks a little more hopeful but is still worried as she watches her mom look from the pink buttons to the metal ones. I give Lizzie her Black Canary button. She whispers, "Thanks."

Crystal leaves with the metal buttons and a very happy daughter. I don't think Lizzie even cares what the dress looks like when finished, just that it isn't going to be pink like all of her other homemade outfits.

Chapter Fourteen

Nurture your mind with great thoughts; to believe in the heroic makes heroes. —Benjamin Disraeli

THE BUTTONS AND OUR Circle of Strength are working out well for all of us. Lizzie is wearing her new outfit to school today. The navy-blue jacket has the buttons that I sold to Crystal, and the red plaid skirt that matches has two buttons at the waist. Lizzie has never looked happier.

I have been spending all my allowance on new clothes and trying my best to look presentable. I am wearing a gray wool pleated skirt with the scarlet turtleneck that my Sweet Betty Sue knitted for me. With our socks pulled to our knees, red headbands, and black Mary Jane shoes, Lizzie and I seem to be turning a lot of heads at school today.

It gives me the extra confidence that I need. I still feel awkward wearing skirts lately, but having Lizzie help me choose the styles and colors makes it easier for me.

After lunch, we meet up with the boys and head into English class. Before we even reach our seats, the teacher taps the board with her long stick of chalk.

"You have ten minutes to prepare an oral presentation on what being a hero means to you." She taps on the board again and says, "Begin now."

After ten minutes, we are instructed to set our pencils down. We take turns reading our essays, beginning alphabetically from the letter Z. I am surprised to hear what the class can produce in such a short amount of time. C.E. is first, and he talks about Superman, the little actions that make big differences, and, of course, how soldiers in past wars and current wars are his heroes.

Lizzie takes her turn before me because she whispers to me that she is nervous and wants to get it over with. She reads her essay about friends who help without questioning, how a comment can brighten a person's day, and how the kindness of others toward her family has felt like an act of heroism to her. I am last because Georgia Adams did not show up to school today.

I stand to read my essay, and my hands start to sweat. "To be a hero, one must maintain good thoughts and do great things, not because it is expected of them, but because they believe it will start a chain reaction of greatness to others around them. Anyone can be a hero. Anyone can be a villain. Everyone has a choice. A hero is someone who is good and never changes; they are someone who maintains optimism when all seems lost. A hero is a soldier who runs into battle while others run away. A hero is not afraid of who they are and can help those in need see that courage lies within them if they are ready to seek it out.

"Of course, my grandpa will always be my hero. Even though he is gone, his legacy of kindness and heroism will be an inspiration to me throughout my life. I also acknowledge the young heroes, those who are trying to become their own heroes through hard work, courage, and strength. Even the smallest act of kindness can be a heroic act to the person receiving it. My grandpa's actions in life taught me that being an example of goodness can inspire others to be heroes. That is what heroism means to me," I say and sit back down.

The room is quiet. Did I have something in my teeth? The bell rings to let school out for the day. I walk out with Lizzie, but Mrs. Stein holds me back.

"Missy, you should think about joining the debate and speech team. They meet every Tuesday after school. Think about it. Penny Copperfield is the president. I know she would love having you on the team," she says and hands me a signed note to give to Penny.

I meet up with C.E. and Lizzie and ask them what they think about Mrs. Stein's suggestion. They both agree that I should join.

"I'm glad I went first. I would not have given my speech if I had to go after you. You have a talent," Lizzie says without malice or bitterness. I know at this moment we have become good friends.

***

By March, the debate team has won three debates in the County division, and I placed fourth in the Original Prose and Poetry Contest.

The Monday afternoon meetings of the Justice League of America are a good way for me to try out my new material and debate tactics. Zeke is always willing to take the opposite side of the debate and is always the first one to clap when I read my prose out loud. Everyone is very supportive and comes to all my conferences.

Today, March 26, is the last day of spring break, and I have the State Debate Championship. I am extremely nervous. Penny, Charlie, and Phillip are talking in a circle behind the curtain on the stage. I peek out to see C.E., Lizzie, Nick, Zeke, and Heck in the front row. Dine, Sweet Betty Sue, Crystal, and Leonard sit behind them with Mrs. Hill and Mrs. Copperfield. C.E. notices me, and he nudges everyone. They all wave to me and lift sheets of paper against their chests that spell out "Go Ogdenville," but Heck's paper is upside down, making me laugh. C.E. mouths "Good luck," and Lizzie crosses her fingers.

I turn to talk with my team and start to shake. I cannot believe we are in the university's main auditorium. All the seats are full. It is great to see all the support, but it doesn't do me any good to see that the place is packed, especially since most of them aren't here to see us. Twenty other schools are competing and four other debates after ours. I start to breathe in through my nose and out my mouth. Phillip stands by my side and mimics me. I move my eyes in his direction and smile.

"That worked. Thanks," he says as I continue to breathe. He tips his head to the side and squints at me. "My Martian Manhunter mind-reading abilities tell me you are nervous beyond explanation," he says, touching his fingertips to my temples.

Phillip is the most handsome boy in school. He has been C.E.'s comic book friend for years, and now I have been on the debate team with him for six months. We have spent a lot of time together either with C.E. or with the debate team. He rubs my temples, and my breathing slows. I close my eyes. When I have calmed down, I look up into his eyes. He is so dreamy to look at that I cannot tell if I am getting nervous again because of the debate or because he is giving me attention.

"Thanks, that worked," I copy him and laugh. His fingertips are still on my temples. He looks into my eyes, and his face is inches from mine. I can smell his cinnamon gum on his breath.

"Your eyes," he says. "What is your heritage?"

"Excuse me?" I say quite shocked. "I don't know what you mean."

"Oh, I'm sorry. I did not mean to offend you. You have really pretty eyes, that's all." He clears his throat and goes to gather his portfolio.

I walk to Penny but cannot stop thinking about my eyes. They are the same as Lizzie's eyes. Heritage? What did that mean? Penny notices that I am distracted.

"This is no time for nerves, Missy Lou. Focus," she says. She grabs my hands and pulls me to the table. She points to the poster that shows our statistics and points of debate. I can hear the announcer at the pulpit. "Phillip, Charlie. Let us do this," she says without stuttering.

We all place our fists in a circle and touch hands. We look at each other in the huddle. Charlie has a determined look on his face. "We're going to win this year. I can feel it. We worked hard and are prepared. No fear," he says as the curtains rise. We bump fists once more.

As team captain, Charlie walks up to the announcer and is introduced to the other team captain. They shake hands and do a coin toss. He walks back to us and says, "We go on last. Get your notepads out and have a rebuttal for everything they say."

We sit at our table, listen, and wait. We debate for thirty minutes, and now it is time for me to give the concluding argument.

"It is human nature to be afraid of the magnitude of evaluating all of the needs in the world. But when it is in your own country, how can you consciously put up a wall, sealing those who need help the most to live a life of suffering under the oppression of the Communist Party?

"The Berlin Wall has only been enforced for four years, but this hasn't stopped East Germans from risking their lives to cross over for a much safer, better life for them-selves and their families. Germany should stop direct-ing their forces to try to keep its fellow countrymen and women from crossing and instead look at the reasons why they are fleeing and seeking refuge in the first place.

"As long as the world tries to divide people, there will always be those who will never give up. The harder it is to cross the wall; the harder people will work to tear it down. The more they exist in suffering, the more they will alter their minds and attitudes to find a way to bring about change.

"Every discouragement can turn into a possibility. It is human nature to have the capacity for decency and goodness, even under the most adverse circumstances. If there is a wall, there will be the hope that one day it will fall."

I finish the speech that we prepared and walk back to the team. We sit and wait for the announcer to receive the envelope from the judges. As soon as he announces Ogdenville as the winner of the debate, we all scream.

"We did it!" Charlie yells as we all hug each other. Phillip comes over, picks me up, and swings me around. He holds on to me a little longer while my arms are still around his neck. C.E. walks up behind us and does not seem the least bit bothered. Lizzie, however, raises her eyebrows and smiles at me.

After pictures and flowers, we meet at a restaurant for dinner. Phillip seems to be giving me a lot of attention, but for some reason, the dreamiest boy in school does not make me feel like I have a dozen butterflies in my stomach. I do not want to give him attention just to try and make C.E. jealous, so I graciously decline his offer to attend the spring dance next month.

I sit in bed and stare at the trophy sitting on the desk, and I look at the picture of my mom with her trophy. It is my first real connection to her. I wish I could see her face better. What did her eyes look like? I feel so self-conscious now.

The clocks chime one a.m. I cannot sleep. I move to the telescope and look out my window toward C.E.'s house. He is still up reading. Most likely reading the latest comics. I notice Phillip and Leonard are there too. I feel sick in my stomach now. I wonder if they are talking about me. I wonder if they are all talking about whomever they each like. Ugh. I am going to bed.

Chapter Fifteen

If we could read the secret history of our enemies, we should find in each man's life sorrow and suffering enough to disarm all hostility. —Henry Wadsworth Longfellow

MARCH 26, 1966

Dear Missy Lou,

Yesterday my wife, Sanjula Nagina Lahiri, gave birth to our son. You have a baby brother. His name is Naji. We will send pictures soon.

Sincerely,

Daniel L. Button

"Did you read this?" I ask my Sweet Betty Sue, completely infuriated. She nods and lifts her letter over her toast. "Well?" I say, hoping to get a reaction. She shrugs her shoulders and takes her plate to the sink. "Today is May 18th, and it's dated in March! You'd think with something this important he could manage to get the letter here earlier than today!" I cannot calm myself down.

"I have to run some buttons into Orville City. I will be back by lunch," she says as she gathers her belongings. She leans over and kisses my head. "It's Saturday. You should be out with your friends. Dine is here to watch the store while I am gone. You may have the cookies in the pantry."

I call C.E. as soon as she leaves. "It's me, Missy. Assemble the Circle at the Watch Tower. I need help now," I say. He hangs up immediately. I grab the cookies and head for the treehouse. Howard runs by my side and tries to catch the grasshoppers that leap from the grass.

I have not seen my dad in almost nine years. He did not even tell me he was married. He alluded to it in one of his letters, but now I only find out for sure because they have had a baby together. How dare he go off and start a new family instead of spending time on the one he already has here in Ogdenville.

Why did he go to India in the first place? Why has he never visited me? Why do I feel like I am not a part of anything anymore? I feel he is choosing a new life and child over me. Now he will never even have a reason to come back home and visit. My world is ending.

A baby? I cannot believe it. A new wife? Does she speak English? Does she know anything about me? I feel the abandonment that I felt when he left for the first time, telling me that he had to go away for a while. He said he needed time. He said he needed to figure out his life. I think time only pushed him further away from me and the button factory. And now I have lost hope.

When we reach the treehouse, there are already three bikes on the lawn, and C.E. is loading up the bucket with drinks to pull up to the top.

"We're all here," he says. He notices the letter sticking out of my pocket. "A letter day, huh?" he says, pulling the rope to the bucket.

I reach the top of the treehouse at the same time as the drinks. I unload and pass them around before placing the bag of cookies in the middle. C.E. climbs up and sits next to me.

"It's a letter day, and it must be pretty bad if we all need to be here," he says.

Everyone is looking at me, waiting for the news. They look as if they are preparing to hear the worst. But when I read the letter, Lizzie groans and rolls her eyes.

"Is that all? So you have a brother. Big deal. I have two!" Lizzie takes a long drink of her cola and looks around the room for support.

I sit completely shocked and speechless. C.E. starts to say something but is interrupted.

"Don't mind her. She's having a bad hair day," Zeke says, and Heck laughs.

"It's not a bad hair day," she snaps. "Missy just needs to grow up and stop playing the pathetic baby. You want and expect everyone to feel sorry for you because your mom's dead and your dad abandoned you. Well, everybody has problems. You should be glad for the family and friends you do have instead of getting everyone worked up over your stupid letter days! Maybe if you sent him letters and tried to put forth some effort in your relationship with him, he might take more interest in you!"

C.E. again tries to say something, but Lizzie throws her cookie at him on her way out of the treehouse. I rise to follow her, but Zeke grabs my hand and yells, "Lizzie Vanilla Bennett, come back here!"

I try again to get up but Zeke squeezes my hand, and I sit back down. "Please don't. She needs to be alone," he says as he watches her run down the road. He is still holding my hand and when I look down at it, he quickly lets it go.

Zeke sits back down, and C.E. and I look to him for answers. He shrugs his shoulders, so we both look at Heck, who lets out a deep breath as if he had been holding it in all day. He shakes his head before lowering it so that we cannot see his face. Zeke clears his throat a few times as if he is about to say something, but he does not.

After a few more minutes, I slap my knees and begin to get up to follow Lizzie.

"Wait. I'll tell you what's going on," Zeke gives in. I sit back down and wait. Heck starts playing with his shoelaces as soon as Zeke starts talking.

"It's our dad," he admits. I realize that I have never met him, never asked about him, and know nothing more than his last name.

"He's out of jail," he quietly says. He looks at Heck, whose head is still bent down and whose nose is holding a few tears steady at its tip.

Both C.E. and I gasp. We had no idea. I feel foolish for causing such drama over a baby being born, and C.E. looks out the treehouse, searching for Lizzie.

I wait for Zeke to continue. He clears his throat again. "My dad used to beat up my mom and us. One night, my mom was beaten up badly, and I hid Heck and Lizzie with me in the closet so my dad couldn't find us. I reached for the phone and dialed the first number on the list that was taped to the receiver. It was your dad that picked up," he says, looking right at me.

I wonder why my dad's number would be at the top of the list at their home, and now I am curious what my dad did.

"Your dad came over and confronted my dad at the front door. He said the police were on their way and not to put up a fight. You were sitting in the car and were screaming, 'Don't hurt my daddy. Please don't hurt my daddy.' You were only five. When the police arrived, your dad had calmed down ours, and they both sat on the porch waiting.

"While the police arrested him, your dad went in to help my mom. He called an ambulance and took all three of us home for the weekend. My dad was sent to jail, and my mom and we have slowly tried to recover. Until today," he finishes, relieved to have it off his chest. However, he seems embarrassed now, and he is hesitant to look at us.

Heck looks up with anger in his face and punches his fist into his palm. "If he ever hurts my mom or us again, I'll kill him," he says through clenched teeth.

"Where is he now? C.E. asks.

"Well, Mom divorced him while he was in jail, so he won't be coming home. She keeps assuring us that he is headed out west for work," Zeke explains. "I can tell she's scared. Lizzie is scared too."

"We better go look for Lizzie. Let's split up," C.E. says urgently, taking command. "No time to waste. Zeke, search the drugstore. Heck, search your house. I will take the school, and Missy, you go to the church. Search the surrounding areas as well." He tells us to meet back here in one hour to regroup and looks at all of us, waiting for us to get on our bikes and go.

On my way to the southeast corner of town, I feel an overwhelming change inside of me. I begin to understand my Sweet Betty Sue's reaction to the letter. Why am I so worked up about my letter day, and why did I think I had the right to cause such a scene over it in the first place?

I felt so small and insignificant the moment I heard their story.

The circle around my little world cracks and dissolves as I pedal as fast as I can to the church. My life collides with the lives of those around me whom I love. It gives me a sense of awareness and sadness, a relief and a burden, but also closeness to and an appreciation for my friends.

There is no sign of her at the church. I park my bike and walk around to the cemetery. I find Lizzie sitting on the wall facing the church, staring at a large, winged statue. I pick a few flowers that line the wall and sit up next to her. She keeps her face focused on the statue. I swing my legs in time with hers, waiting for her to talk to me. We watch Howard try and catch butterflies among the wildflowers.

She blows her bangs out of her face and stops swinging her legs. "I have always been so jealous of you. I have hated you since I could remember, probably around five years old. Your dad came to rescue my mom, my brothers, and me from my dad. He had been beating us for years. We stayed with you a few days while my mom was recuperating at the hospital. The first time I got jealous of you is when I watched your dad put you to bed one night. He sang to you some silly song, and you giggled. He checked on you three times during the night."

"I don't remember any of that. I'm sorry," I say, trying to hide the sadness in my voice.

"I think I remember it because it was so traumatic. It was my pain. It was my dad who went to jail, while you were being sung lullabies and tickled by yours. "She wipes her tears and reaches out to grab my hand. "I'm sorry I said those things. I shouldn't have called you a baby."

"No, you're right. I have a dad." I look up at the statue and marvel at its wingspan. "I complain every time he sends me a letter, but I never write to him. How can I expect him to open up to me if I don't let him know anything about me and what I am doing?" I say, pulling the petals off the flowers. "I haven't seen him in years, but I know he loves me. And now I have a little brother. I need to stop feeling as if I have been wronged in that situation because I am the one who built the wall up between us."

Lizzie takes the flowers from my hands and tucks a few in my hair. I place the remaining flowers in hers. We hop off the wall and take one more look at the large, winged statue.

"Do you visit this statue often?" I ask as we walk away.

She looks back at it. "My mom loves it. She sits underneath it and reads on the weekends. I come here when I am looking for her, that's all. It seemed a good place to clear my head today."

I take her hand as we walk back to my bike. "Hop on," I say.

As we ride back to the Watch Tower, Lizzie suggests, "Maybe we can make a little package of goodies for Naji. And maybe send a belated wedding present to your dad and Sanjula.

"Good idea," I say. "And by the way, my middle name is Nutmeg. I think it's interesting that yours is Vanilla." I continue to pedal as Lizzie holds on to my shoulders.

She looks down at my face as I look up. "Maybe our moms were friends," she says, and the idea makes us both laugh.

Chapter Sixteen

We relish news of our heroes, forgetting that we are extraordinary to somebody too. —Helen Hayes

SCHOOL HAS BEEN OUT for nearly two months now. If it were not for my birthday in two days, I would be completely bored and ready for school to start again.

I have missed my debate team but given the load of research and assignments to outline, I have been busy this summer. C.E. and I have been sitting at the creek like we usually do. The Bennetts have been bussed off to different camps for the summer. Lizzie will not be back in time for my birthday. Since we have become friends this past year, I learned that her birthday was last week, but she has already been gone for two weeks. I sent her a framed picture of us from the Halloween dance dressed as superheroes and a box of her favorite chocolates. I cannot wait until she gets back. We will only have two weeks to shop for school.

My Sweet Betty Sue is being extra sneaky about my birthday this year. She asked Ms. Tovah Stein if she could take me to the orthodontist, which is in Orville City where she works. Sweet Betty Sue never asks favors of others, but I was even more shocked when the offer that Ms.

Tovah Stein presented to Sweet Betty Sue was accepted without a blink.

"I have a better idea. My home is being fumigated for termites, and I have a hotel for two days in downtown Orville City. Why doesn't Missy Lou stay the weekend with me? I will get her back on her birthday." She did not even have to persuade my Sweet Betty Sue. I guess turning fourteen already has its rewards.

Our first day in the city is spent at the orthodontist, where I finally get my braces off. I know C.E. will be jealous when he sees that I got mine off before him, so I ask for a sparkly toothbrush to take home for him. He will not get his off for a while. Since the accident, they had to tighten his teeth and put an extra metal strap on his braces. It will be another year or two before his can come off. I hope he likes the sparkles on his new toothbrush.

After we leave the orthodontist's office on the fringe of the city, we drive into the heart of downtown. I have only been to the orthodontist and never in the actual city. I have never had any reason to until today. With the windows rolled down, I stick my arm out and test how close my hand can get to the cars parked on the streets. I look up at the towering buildings and watch the people hurrying in and out of them like ants.

Glamorous shops are lining the streets, with mannequins dressed in Chanel and Gucci. We slowly pull into a covered valet tent in front of a beautiful hotel. A man opens my door, and Ms. Tovah Stein and I get out.

"Room 204, please," she says. I stand outside the car and look at the building. She links her arm in mine and leads me through the doors, which are held open by the concierge. "Thank you," she says with an almost Hollywood–like flair. I am speechless.

After we eat dinner in the hotel restaurant, we head upstairs where our luggage is waiting in the room. There is a vase of roses on the desk near the veranda and an envelope with my name on it. I claim the bed by the windows, and Ms. Tovah Stein eats the mint left for her on her pillow. "What's in the envelope?" she asks as she takes the mint from my bed and eats it too.

I open it, and there are two tickets to the Philharmonic tonight with "Guest Performer: Eva Meadows, Pianist, featuring the works of Gershwin."

"I told Crystal I was taking you downtown for the weekend, and she pulled a few strings with Eva. Crystal made her performance gown in exchange for those tickets." As she gets up, her bracelets jingle.

"You could play in the symphony with all those bracelets," I tease. She laughs and moves to the desk. I watch her examine the skin underneath her bracelets. She presses on her rough skin and wrings her wrists. It never occurred to me that the reason she wears so many bracelets is that she is hiding something. I decide not to ask. She must have a reason for not telling me.

"Should we put your hair in curlers for tonight?" she asks as she pulls makeup, jewelry, and hair accessories from her bag.

***

The next morning, I think about the amazing concert last night. Eva Meadows played wonderfully. I want to ask my Sweet Betty Sue for piano lessons when I get home later today.

As Ms. Tovah Stein and I eat breakfast, I cannot stop talking about how glamorous and talented Eva was last night.

"How is your quiche?" she asks.

"It's pretty fancy. I have never had anything like it. It looks like something C.E. would be allergic to," I say as I play with my food. "I remember the day we found out he is allergic to peanut butter. We were eight, and Mrs. Parker gave us a tablespoon of peanut butter to suck on to keep quiet while she played bridge with my Sweet Betty Sue. He swelled up so fast ..." I trail off when I notice that she is looking across the room at something.

She gasps and points. "Oh my gosh, there's C.E. now!" I jump out of my seat and smile from ear to ear, frantically looking around. When I realize that he is not there, I look back at Ms. Tovah Stein and stick my tongue out at her for tricking me.

She wipes the corner of her mouth delicately with her napkin and looks at me as if she is waiting for me to tell her a secret. "You were saying something about C.E. and peanut butter," she says, leaning her head on her hands with her elbows planted on the table. She blinks wildly at me.

"I wonder if he will be there for my birthday this afternoon," I say, looking to her for reassurance.

"Why do you doubt him?" she asks, and I am taken aback because I expected that she would soothe me with promises that he will always be there for me.

I press my shoulders back against my chair. "I don't doubt him. I sometimes regret wishing he had become the person I always knew he could be. He has changed a lot. I guess I can't expect him to always be around," I say and then pause to play with the charm she gave me last year. I give in to a little smile. "I don't regret wishing anything when it comes to C.E. Watching him this last year turn into his own hero, my hero, and a good friend to so many makes me happy. If that means I have to let him go, hoping he will still be my friend, then that's all I could wish for now."

"That is the truest form of love: to want what's best for someone even if it means losing them. Well done, Missy," she says as she takes my hand, and we leave the restaurant.

As we walk to the valet, she squeezes my hand. "I wouldn't doubt him. If he is anything like his father, his love for those in his life runs deep and true too."

She shakes my wrist, and it jingles like hers. She notices the charm bracelet and says, "Oh, I'm glad to see that you wear that slipper. It's a key." She winks at me.

"A key?" I inspect it closer. I jump when the valet slams the car door shut

"The stories I could tell you," she says with a laugh and accidentally hits the car horn. "Maybe one day I will tell you about that charm, but for now, you're expected back home."

The trip home is only a twenty-minute drive. While Ms. Tovah Stein sings along to the radio, I realize that since I was away from home on my birthday, I did not wake to the clocks chiming at six a.m. After being wooed by the city for two days, I feel homesick. I think of my grandpa's birthday wish speech and realize why he loved our town so much. I hear his voice again, and it makes me happy: "That whitewashed house with baby blue shutters, the barn, the brick button factory that towers over and protects our home, the tall trees, the geranium lined dirt road. Ah, the covered bridge over Thimble Creek, the train station at the edge of town. A town that offers anything you could ever need. Amazing."

I can see Ogdenville in the distance, including my grandpa's "eight necessities a town needs: a church, a school, a hospital, a library, a movie theater, a corner market, a drugstore, and a paint store. Not to forget a pretty nice button factory, of course." I realize that I created the change in myself this year. The loss I feel for my grandpa has turned to comfort as I look on the town he adored, a town that I now cannot live without. My anger from his absence has dissolved to peace as I cherish all the wonderful memories

I have of him, and I have found happiness in the things that gave him joy.

When we reach my driveway, Ms. Tovah Stein slows the car to a stop and hugs me. I grab my suitcase and say, "Thanks for everything. The city is fantastic, but I understand now why you and my grandpa always talk about our town as being the only place to live."

"I knew one day you'd feel the same. I will never leave. I will always be here," she says and honks her horn. "Happy birthday, Missy Lou," she shouts over the loud music.

I skip to the back door where I hope C.E. is waiting to ask me to go fishing. I throw my suitcase down on the table when out from the pantry jump C.E., Dine, and my Sweet Betty Sue.

"Happy birthday," they shout. Howard barks and jumps up on my dress.

I smile big, and they gasp. I forgot they have not seen me without my braces yet. Dine walks over to me, kisses my cheek, and hands me a large bouquet of daisies. "You look beautiful," he whispers.

After I hug Sweet Betty Sue, we settle at the table for angel food cake and whipped cream.

Here. Open it, and then I can explain the rest of your gift," Sweet Betty Sue says. I open a large box wrapped in baby blue paper. Inside is the most exquisite quilt. It is cream with embroidered red roses and daisies with green vines and leaves. Of course, there are several beautiful buttons for the middles of all the flowers. I hug her and thank her. "For the rest of your gift, we will redecorate your bedroom. It is about time. I have already ordered the wallpaper, paint, and a new headboard. We will start on it next week."

I have never asked to fix my room up. The thought makes me happy.

"Thank you. And thank you, Dine, for the daisies. I always love daisies on my birthday. They are such a happy flower," I say. I turn to C.E., who looks bashful.

"I'll give you your gift at the creek," he says before shoving a large bite of cake in his mouth.

I lean closer and notice a large black dot above his lip. I look at his fingers, and they are also covered in black ink. "Uh, C.E., you have a blob of black ink on your face." He wipes it with his finger, forgetting that it too is covered in ink, and he smears a black line above his top lip, making himself look like he has a handlebar mustache. We all start to laugh, and he runs to the sink to clean it off.

"There's rubbing alcohol next to the talcum powder in the cupboard under the sink," Sweet Betty Sue says. When he places the bottle of rubbing alcohol back, he knocks the powder down, and it falls on his head.

I throw my head back and laugh. After all the changes that C.E. has made this year, he is still accident-prone. "This reminds me of our fourth-grade summer when we were cooped up in the house." I start to tell the story about the baby powder, but he throws his towel at me and heads for the bathroom.

"I don't want to hear it!" He laughs as he closes the bathroom door.

Sweet Betty Sue wipes her eyes with her apron. She looks to Dine, who is wiping his face with his handkerchief. "You kids could have suffocated!" she says through tears. "I still cannot believe you used an entire bottle of baby powder as snow in your bedroom. I remember hearing 'It's snowing, it's snowing,' broken up by two little coughs over and over. When we walked in, a plume of white dust hit us in the face. Your grandpa threw open the window and hung your bodies outside it."

C.E. walks back into the kitchen with a wet head and no sign of talcum powder. "Snow in the middle of summer was your idea. I can't stand the smell of baby powder, thanks to you," he says as he slugs my arm. He does not hit me hard, but it stings all the same. My laugh fades, and I sweetly smile at him. He takes the last piece of cake before I can and stuffs it in his mouth.

"Oh! By the way," Sweet Betty Sue says, "Lizzie dropped this off before she left for camp a few weeks ago and told me to wait until your birthday to give it to you." She hands me a small box tied with a red ribbon.

Inside is a framed picture of the two of us at the State Debate Conference. We have our arms over each other's shoulders, and I am holding the large bouquet of daisies Dine had brought me that day. Our heads are touching. At a glance, we almost look like sisters. It makes me smile to remember that day, and I miss Lizzie.

"This came today too," Sweet Betty Sue says, handing me a letter.

I know it's from my dad by the return address. It is the first year that I have received my birthday letter on time from him.

I open the envelope, and a delicate charm falls out. I put it on my bracelet next to the slipper charm that Ms. Tovah Stein gave me, and I read the letter.

Dear Missy Lou,

Happy Birthday. Sanjula found this charm at the market and thought you would like it. I sent your college fund check to your grandma, and I have enclosed pictures of Naji. At five months old, he only blows bubbles when he tries to talk, but I think his first word will be Missy. He loved the toys you sent, and he carries your picture everywhere he goes.

Keep up the good work in debate and speech. We will send more items from India to introduce you to the culture here. I hope you will love it as much as I do if you ever decide to visit.

Love,

Daniel, Sanjula, and Naji

P.S. Your charm is Sarasvati, the goddess of knowledge, wisdom, and art. Her name means "The Flowing One." She is the goddess of knowledge and the originator of speech and all the arts.

I look at the charm, a woman with multiple arms, and the pictures of my half-brother.

"Let's go fishing," C.E. says after he gulps down a full glass of milk.

I smile. I was hoping that we would go fishing today. I slug him on the arm as I get up from the table. "Let me change into my overalls and I'll be right down," I say.

My Sweet Betty Sue follows me to my room.

It smells like paint as I walk up the stairs. I look up at the landing and see Dandelion, Ethel, Rosie, and Nancy Jo leaning on the banister. "Hello, ladies," I say with suspicion rising in my voice as I say the word *ladies*.

"Hi," they all casually say and walk into Sweet Betty Sue's bedroom. The sight of four plump, purple-haired ladies in polyester dresses makes me laugh.

I walk into my room. "Oops, wrong room," I say and turn to leave. I stop and spin around. "What? My room!" I scream ecstatically. "Grandma!" She is already in my doorway.

"Happy birthday, Missy," she timidly says. I run to her and embrace her. I have forgotten how soft and thin her skin is, how she smells of beauty powder, how her curls softly bounce on my face, and how fragile she is.

"Now, now. All right," she says while smoothing her apron. I can tell she does not want to get emotional.

"How did you do this?" I ask.

"I hope you like it," she says as she fluffs the pillows on my bed.

I touch my new quilt and say, "I love it." I look around and take in all the beautiful new things in my room. I notice the red gingham wallpaper. My headboard is white, and it matches my nightstand, dresser, and desk. My telescope is in the same place as before, just on a new desk. I lift it and look out the window to see C.E. reach his front door.

The daisies Dine gave me are on my nightstand, and my picture from Lizzie is on my desk. I look and find the picture of my parents on the wall by my Cheval mirror, along with a picture of the Justice League, one of my grandpa holding me as a toddler, and one of C.E. and myself fishing down at the creek. I move the door a little bit to see two more pictures. One is of my Sweet Betty Sue cradling me in the rocker when I was born, and the other is a group of six friends I don't recognize.

I take the frame down and stare at it. I notice my mom and my dad. Then, I recognize Dine. Sweet Betty Sue quietly walks up behind me and looks over my shoulder. "The other three are Ms. Tovah Stein, Crystal, and Barty Stein. This was taken before Dine and Barty left for the war in 1944. They were seniors in high school."

I take the picture down for a closer look at it. Crystal is on my dad's back making bunny ears behind his head. Dine has his hand on my mom's shoulder, and Bart is kissing Ms. Tovah Stein on the cheek.

"They were all very close friends," she says and takes the frame from my hands. She carefully turns it over and pulls off a folded piece of paper. She hands it to me and sits down on my bed.

I follow her and open it. "A treasure map? What kind of treasure? The Justice League will love this!" I look at the clues, all the names on it. Everyone from the picture signed his or her name. I touch the signature of my mother. I have never seen her handwriting before. "Mama," I whisper as I turn the frame back over and look at the picture.

"Her friends made a promise to watch over you the day you were born. She knew she was not going to make it. The morning before you were born, they all met one last time. 'Nothing binds us one to the other like a promise kept. Nothing divides us like a promise broken' was their motto. I think they got it from a Mutual Life Insurance Company flyer from the bank. Anyway, they have kept that promise, each watching over you in their own way." She pulls the hair back out of my face. As I start to cry, she hands me her handkerchief.

All these years, my mother's friends have protected me, loved me, and guided me. I have loved them as if they were family, and now I know I was right in doing so. My heart feels light but also a little like a weight is pressing down on it. "Mama," I whisper again and touch her signature.

"I know that it's hard not knowing who your mom was and having your dad gone halfway around the world," Sweet Betty Sue admits. She tightens up and places her fists on her knees. "I have been so wrong all these years not to talk to you about your mother. There were a lot of reasons, but none that should keep me from letting you know about her now." She stands up and says, "Come with me." She takes my hand and leads me to the attic.

She unlocks the door. "This will remain unlocked from now on. I shouldn't have kept you from the memory of your grandpa, no matter how hard it is for me." We walk in, and I feel my grandpa's love for me as I touch his books and war medals. I can smell his old pipe sitting on the dresser. Sweet Betty Sue points to my mother's hope chest.

She holds out a small key and places it in my hand. "We find out who we are by looking to the past for answers. Who we are is a perpetual work in progress, always looking back, always looking forward. Who we are is an ideal that we aim for in life.

"You are your grandpa. You are your mother. You are a piece of every family member who came before you. You reflect the goodness in your friends. Who you are is a beautiful balance of everyone in your life. And without you in our lives, we would all be missing something important, like the stars would miss the moon. Live a good life because you too will pass on a piece of yourself to future generations," she says and walks me over to the chest. "Everything you've wanted to know about your mother is in there, waiting." She touches the side of my face before leaving me alone with the chest.

I kneel before it and touch the carved red roses on the front of it. The initials are CPS, which confuses me. I slowly open the lid, and I see my reflection in the mirror attached to the inside of it. Next to it is a photograph of my mother at my age.

I can hear the voice from the dream last year on my birthday. *My little miss, hush now. I am here.*

I lift a certificate from the top of a pink afghan. It is her death certificate. Cause of death: Cardiomyopathy.

I hear the singing of my mother. *Soft as the voice of an angel.... Hope for the sunshine tomorrow... Whispering hope... Making my heart in its sorrow rejoice.*

Here, on my fourteenth birthday, I discover my mother and her dying love for me. Was she too not a hero by giving birth to me, knowing she would not live? For what is a hero without hope?

I was her hope.

I lift my birth certificate, which sits next to her death certificate. Shivers crawl up my spine as I realize that both certificates were filled out on the same day. I look at my mother's name, Gemma Lovely Sholes. I look next to her name, which lists her ethnicity. It reads Japanese American. My heart skips a beat. I look at my mother's picture again and then at myself.

On the death certificate at the bottom, there is a signature for the release of the body: *Crystal Pretty Bennett, Sister.* I look at the front of the hope chest and touch the initials CPS. This is Crystal's hope chest. Where is my mother's? I start to panic. This is too much information for me to receive all at once.

My heart pounds in my chest. I must see Crystal. I cannot wait. I place the papers back in the chest and notice my mother's handwriting. I pick the paper up and sit up against the hope chest.

It is a library index card with all the books from June 1952 that she checked out. They are all about the heart, heart transplants, new medical breakthroughs, and medications. On the back, she wrote a poem that I think I remember C.E. reading to me from my dad's old book.

I close the hope chest and decide to finish looking through it another day after I have had time to digest all the information I have just learned. I have so many questions. My priority will be to visit Crystal. I have an aunt! And that means that Lizzie is my cousin! I have a family! I grab the library card with the poem on it and hold it next to my heart. I sigh.

Howard runs up next to me with a note attached to his collar. I scratch behind his ears and kiss the top of his head before reading the note.

Dear W.W.,

Meet me downstairs. Your invisible airplane waits to take you to the creek. Your you-know-what is wrapped and waiting to be opened.

Hurry up, birthday girl.

Love, S.M. (simply me)

When we reach the creek, C.E. pulls a thin package out of his overalls. We sit down on the log and position our poles to catch fish. While I open the gift, C.E. places worms on our hooks.

There is a new red bandana folded neatly. I tie it around my head and look over at C.E. He pulls a strand of loose hair and tucks it behind my ear. I look down to see what was under the bandana. It's a homemade comic book. The front cover has a superhero in a silver bodysuit, silver visor, and red cape. There is a red lightning bolt on his chest and the sides of his shiny helmet. The comic is titled *Captain Steel Spine and the Capture of the Key*. I look up from the comic and notice C.E. is blushing. I can tell he has put a lot of thought and time into this. He looks away and pricks his finger with the hook. I grab his hand.

"This is amazing. Thank you. I was wanting to get a new bandana too," I say as I dab his finger with a napkin from the tackle box that was sitting next to our apples. I hesitate a little before I tell him what I found in the attic. I want to tell him everything. I open my mouth to speak, but he moves closer to me, and I stop.

"You've gotten stylish this year and changed a lot. But there is something about that red bandana and your old painting overalls that makes me happy," he says. He sucks on his finger and looks out over the creek. "I guess it makes me feel like we aren't growing up too fast. I don't want to miss anything."

I look down at the comic book. "Will you read it to me?" I ask. He simply nods, still looking down. I think he is embarrassed and afraid of my reaction to the story. He knows I have always been his biggest supporter in everything he does, but somehow today he seems bashful around me.

He takes the comic from my hands and finally looks at me. I point to the cover's illustrations. "You've progressed in your artwork. Your skill is nearly mastered. I'm impressed," I compliment him, which seems to do the trick in snapping him out of his quiet state.

"OK. Are you ready?" he asks.

"Yes! Now read it already," I tease as I push him off the log. He lies on the ground with the comic above him. I lay down beside him, my head tilted into his, and he reads his story. Howard rests his head on my stomach.

"Wonder Woman, it's a trap!" Superman yells from the top of the Empire State Building.

But it's too late. The Key has disguised himself as a man in distress, ready to jump to his death off the building. He pleaded for help when he slipped and is dangling from the window on the highest floor.

"Here. Take hold of my lasso," Wonder Woman says. When the Key is pulled to safety, he takes her lasso and ties Wonder Woman to the radio tower.

"The Key!" she screams in horror. She knows that she cannot fight the strength of her own lasso. She is trapped. Who will save her from the psychochemical ray gun that will turn her into a Super Slave? Superman flies to her aid.

Wonder Woman notices kryptonite behind the Key's back. As Superman lands by Wonder Woman's side, she yells, "He has kryptonite!" But again, it is too late. The Key shines it on him, making him weak. The Key ties him up with Wonder Woman.

"There is no one left who can save you," the Key says. He throws his head back and laughs. It echoes through the city. All the people watch in horror as the world's two strongest heroes face their doom.

As the Key charges up the psychochemical ray gun, Superman notices Captain Steel Spine climbing up the building next to them. The Captain jumps from one building to the next, landing behind the Key. "I'll take that," he says, and with one little yank, the Key is stripped of his evil power.

The Key runs away as Captain Steel Spine unties Superman and Wonder Woman from the radio tower. They all glide safely down to the street below, and the crowd cheers. Captain Steel Spine reaches out to remove the kryptonite from Superman so he can regain his strength when a screech comes from the sky.

The Key has dislodged the radio tower, and it is plummeting to earth at a speed faster than Wonder Woman can lasso it and before Superman can regain his strength from the kryptonite.

Now, who will save the people of the city?

As the radio tower is feet away from flattening everyone on the block including the superheroes, Captain Steel Spine transforms into a large sheet of metal, protecting everybody. Crash! The noise reverberates through the city. When the noise stops, everyone cheers. Captain Steel Spine has Superman throw the radio tower into space.

"Thank you, Captain Steel Spine. You saved us!" Wonder Woman cries.

Superman shakes his hand. "What would the world be without Captain Steel Spine? I hope I never find out," he says.

Later that day, Captain Steel Spine reverts to his alter ego, Howard Button, the painter down the road. "Have a busy day today, dear?" his wife asks as she pours him a glass of lemonade.

"Ah, just the usual," he says. He takes a cool drink and smiles.

C.E. closes the comic. We sit up, and I throw rocks into the creek. "Thanks, C.E. This is perfect. My grandpa would have loved it. Just like I love it. You are talented. The graphics are amazing. I can't wait to show the Justice League at our next meeting at the Watch Tower."

I stand up and take his hands to help him up. I look down to kick loose grass off my shoes.

When I lift my head, C.E. is in front of me, and his face is coming closer to mine. He kisses me but misses me again and kisses my eye as he bonks me on the head. "Ouch." I laugh. I rub my head, and he starts to laugh too.

"I should stop trying. The next time I might get your ear," he admits as he rubs his forehead. He grabs his pole and throws his line out.

I take my pole and stand next to him. I cast my line and move my arm closer, so it touches his. He looks down at me and I look at him with my *I am so in love with you, Cornelius Everblot Zog* look. "Maybe next year?" I say.

He puts his arm around me and pulls me close to him. He lets out a small laugh and sighs. "Yeah. Maybe next year."

When C.E. drops me off at home, it is near twilight. I say, "Lizzie comes home tomorrow. We are going roller-skating. Want to come?"

"No, thanks. I am meeting the guys down at the arcade. Maybe we can meet up later for pizza," he says.

I start kicking at the step and find the courage to tell him about our parents. "C.E. there are a lot of things I need to tell you," I say.

He takes me in his arms and hugs me tenderly.

My chin rests on his shoulder. He has grown a few inches this year, so I have to get up on my tiptoes a bit. He turns and kisses my temple. He holds me there for a moment and whispers in my ear, "I love you, Missy Lou." He tightens his hold on me before slowly moving away.

He traces the scar on my forehead with his thumb. I look up at his scar and trace it with my finger. Our hands meet and we interlace our fingers. He brings our hands to his lips and kisses my knuckles.

My heart races, and it tickles my ribs. "I love you too, Cornelius," I barely whisper.

I play with one of his buttons and ask him, "Can I make you dinner tomorrow night? How does fried chicken sound?" He nods. "I have a lot of interesting things I want to tell you." He is still nodding as though he is not listening to me.

I pull a button off his shirt and step back. He lets a soft laugh out. "For the jar?" he asks.

"Yes, may I have it?" I watch him move closer to me again. He takes a lock of my hair with his pocketknife and ties the fishing line around it.

"May I have this?" he says as he tucks it in his front pocket. We hug one more time before we turn to leave one another.

I run to my room so that I can watch him with my telescope. I play with the newly cut hair next to my ear while I watch for C.E. When he reaches his front door, he waves in front of the porch light so I can see he made it home safely.

I place the treasure map on my nightstand. I cannot wait to show C.E. tomorrow. I hope this map will lead me to my mother's past. I tuck the poem on the library index card in my jar of buttons and baubles and place it next to the map. I place C.E.'s button on my charm bracelet next to my Indian goddess and the silver slipper. I cross my fingers and make a wish. *I hope C.E. and I will always love each other.*

Howard jumps up and lays his head on my pillow. With a click, the light is off, and I pull the covers up around my chin. The clocks are chiming half past midnight.

I think of my mother's favorite poem as I fall asleep, hearing her voice softly whisper Emily Dickinson's words to me.

"Hope is a thing with feathers that perches in
the soul and sings the tune without the words
and never stops at all."

Also by Sara Madden

Children's Picture Books
Jahan Akua
Jun Anzu
Lucy's Umbrella
Pauly & Fluff's Day at the Beach
The Elf Who Didn't Believe in Children
The Kind Kindergarten Class
The Prince's Dress Dilemma
Too

Early Chapter Reader Books
The Adventures of Tallulah Froom Un–Book One
The Adventures of Tallulah Froom Un–Book Two

Author's Websites

www.saramadden.com
www.velvetpumpkinbooks.com

About the author

Sara, who may or may not be a witch, grew up on California's Central Coast. She was raised on donuts and cookies provided by her Keele grandparents' Tan Top Bakery. She wrote her first story at age six, titled "I Love My Family," and she has been writing ever since. Growing up dyslexic (and her continued fun with it into adulthood), Sara always has and always will find comfort in words, imagination, and believing in the unbelievable.

She currently lives in Millcreek, Utah, with her adorable family, who may or may not be completely bonkers. She has four unreliable guard dogs, eight clocks that refuse to tell time, and four unremarkable typewriters. Buttery popcorn and cinnamon cake donuts are her favorite food. In her spare time, she loves to paint and roller-skate, but never at the same time—messes are dangerously unavoidable (she knows; she's tried it!).